Mother cross

Maleen Junge

B
BALLINDINAS PRESS

Published by BALLINDINAS PRESS 2015
Escallonia Heights, Three Rocks Lane
Barntown-Wexford, Ireland
www.ballindinaspress.com

A CIP catalogue record for this book is available
from the British Library

ISBN: 978-0-9933074-0-9

Printed and bound in Great Britain by CPI

For my son Bengt Krauß

Prologue

My son, their grandchild, is sleeping now. He is four months old. I'm taking him to Ireland so they can hold him in their arms. My wife says they are not that old, they could book a flight and come down to Cape Town themselves to see the child. Flying is easy and cheap these days, she says, and if you don't think of the threat of a terrorist attack, travelling by plane is a safe journey. But my mother doesn't like to travel so far. She doesn't like to leave Ireland at all. I really don't know what to think. My father says treat her with care. She is like a glass that had something too hot in it. Now it has a crack. If you touch it, it could break. These are not my father's own words. He found that remark in one of my mother's German books. I believe it's from the philosopher Nietzsche. My father started studying German before I was born. We spoke German at home. Soon he was able to read the books she had brought and what she was writing herself. I can never tell which language I prefer. You are a half breed my mother says sometimes. That's her horse language. I am half Irish and half German. Maybe I don't want to choose a first language and therefore don't choose a favourite country either. I'm living in South Africa now anyway.

The stewardess just admires my son. "What a beautiful baby," she says. "I hope he will sleep through our night flight. You could relax and read your book. Unusual title- what does it mean?"

"I really don't know," I tell her. "It is a novel my mother has written. Her first novel in English."

"And would one notice that the author is German?"

I am amused and answer: "I expect one would gather from her choice of words and here and there from her construction of some sentences. But readers seem to like it anyway. It's selling well."

The stewardess looks at the title of the book lying on the empty seat beside me. I can see that she is intrigued by the cover.

"Let me know if you need anything," she says touching the carrier of the baby in front of me and walks down the aisle.

I pick up a bottle of water and take the book. To be honest I don't understand the meaning of the title myself. 'You will, eventually', my mother said on the phone. So I open the book and start reading.

———

The Leibstandarte Adolf Hitler 1936

She did not know why her mother talked little about her own childhood. But she remembered that her mother had been one of three sisters and her mother was the one who rebelled against her family's petit-bourgeois sense of respectability. That led to occasional rows with her father about boyfriends. In her late twenties her mother was earning her living as a secretary and eventually rented her own room two streets away from the family home. She remembered her mother saying with a high, scornful voice, trembling with old fury: 'When I was leaving my father said: 'Now you'll be able to receive all your admirers.' Her mother must have received her father as well. Her mother never told her if she was engaged to her father and then became pregnant or if the child was on its way first.

However, the lovers had a problem. It was then that her father and mother realized the political circumstances of the thirties in Nazi Germany could be their salvation. Her father was twenty five then, five years younger than his fiancée, a supporter of 'Deutsch National' ideas and unemployed. As far as she knew her father's job as a journalist had come to an end because his Hitler had wound up the newspaper he was working for. Her mother told her twenty years later that large sectors of the press had to close down if their publishers did not believe in the new future Adolf Hitler was promising the nation. Or if they were Jews.

Her parents, she discovered, were not very worried about their problem. Every day on the radio there were promises and descriptions of the glorious days to come. Her father had plans to write for the Stuermer, a newspaper established by the Nazis to promote national socialist ideas. And also to agitate vigorously against the Jews.

Then, one morning in the spring of 1936, as he looked in the mirror while shaving, her father had an inspiration and suddenly felt he knew where he belonged. He took a deep breath, brought his face nearer to the mirror and told himself: "Yes, I come up to all their expectations." Strange to know that this very moment sealed her fate.

Her father went on talking to himself: "Let us check the details. Am I tall? Yes, I am. Am I young, sporty and blond with blue eyes? Oh, yes, I am. And I have certainly got northern blood in my veins. All I have to prove now is that my fiancée is 'Aryan', noble, too. That won't be hard. Thankfully there are no Jews in either of our families."

She believed that, at this point of his considerations, her father was thinking: 'Great! Absolutely great!' And then she pictured him turning around and telling an imagined audience: "I shall apply to join the Leibstandarte Adolf Hitler, the group of Hitler's guards."

Three months later her father and mother moved to Berlin to pay homage to Hitler. They married without any family members or friends present. Her father told his own mother the news in a letter, her mother's family saw it advertised in the local newspaper. Then, full of expectation, they started their new life: He in the barracks of the Leibstandarte and she, after a period in a rented room, as the proud wife of an elite soldier in a brand new apartment on the housing estate of the Leibstandarte in Lichterfelde West. They enjoyed the Olympic Games and all the fuss surrounding them and then came the birth of the nicest baby the world had ever seen. Her sister.

The day she herself arrived, two and a half years later early in the year 1939, was not such a great day of celebration, she later learned. This time her father had expected a boy. A son.

"The Führer needs men," her father exclaimed with real disappointment in his voice.

"But he needs girls as well." Her mother spoke these words rebelliously to overcome the sad feeling her husband's point of view had triggered. "Women are the ones who see that life goes on at home when the men are at war."

"We are not at war."

"Not yet." Now her mother had expressed what everyone feared and spoke about in secret. That there would be a war soon. Nothing else explained why in Berlin many huge bomb shelters were being built. And walls in cellars were broken through to connect terraced houses in case their house was hit during a bombardment. People who looked for protection in their cellar were then able to reach the cellar next door and later the street.

"Then next time," her father said.

"What do you mean?" her mother asked although she was very well aware what these three words meant. But her mother did not want to become pregnant again.

"The next will be a son." Her father spoke as if it was all already sorted. When he saw her mother's disagreeing expression he went on in a less demanding manner: "Well, with the next baby we'll get two things in one." Now he had a smile of conspiracy on his face. "I get my son, I am sure, and shall not be laughed at by my comrades. And the same time you will be honoured with the Mothercross for having given birth to three children. I am determined to fulfil the Führer's wish for more children."

Her mother now had to tell herself that this was her wish too. Had they not come to Berlin to help to build a new Germany with Hitler? And he actually did deserve gratitude. He had given them a roof over their heads and a good salary to live on in beautiful Berlin.

Twenty months later a boy was born and the mother of three proudly received the Mothercross of the Third German Reich. Hitler's war was underway at this time. Poland was attacked, France invaded and England bombarded in preparation of an invasion.

Later she often heard her mother say that her father back then had been happy to achieve his goal and looked forward to achieving more alongside his beloved Führer.

———

The Air-Raid Shelter 1942

It was in Berlin in the spring of 1942 when she, her sister and her brother had to go to bed early one evening. Her mother came to say 'Good night', but did not leave immediately as she usually did.

"We are in a war," her mother said, "Your father is in France. In Paris. He is very busy there and cannot come home often. I have to bear the burden myself. So listen!" Her mother picked up a pair of socks from the floor and put it on top of her brother's trousers beside his bed. Then she went on: "You have to make a tidy pile of your clothes beside your bed every night. So you can get dressed quickly when the air-raid alarm goes off."

She was three years and a few months old and knew that all this had to be done because of the bombs. As soon as the wail of sirens would start in the night they all had do get up, get dressed and hurry to the Leibstandarte air raid shelter. The shelter was a nice building underground. There was a long hallway with a long red carpet and many rooms with bunk beds for the children and chairs for the adults. The mothers and others. She could never sleep in the shelter although her mother wanted her to. She listened to the women talking and sometimes held her breath when there was a certain loud, rolling noise upstairs, outside. She knew houses were crashing down.

"They are bombing innocent women and children," the Leibstandarte mothers told each other, "but Hitler will give them the right answer."

They talked a lot about this man Hitler in the air-raid

shelter. They said he was a very nice man. And he had come to make them a better life. Everyone around where they lived loved him. And her father had said: "One day I shall hand you over to him. He will take you into his arms and kiss you. I promise." She was not sure if she would like that. She did not like the picture of Hitler on the wall in the sitting room. His looks frightened her.

The night her mother had reproved them, the sound of the sirens woke her shortly after she had fallen asleep. Although she dressed herself quickly and properly so that Ruth could concentrate on getting her little brother ready they did not set off to the shelter. Planes could already be heard flying nearby. The four families in their apartment house assembled in the cellar. There were chairs there as well. And the man from downstairs brought water for all of them. Through the small window near the ceiling she could hear the sound of groups of planes, sudden bangs and she could see red, flickering light.

"It is burning nearby," her mother said with her usual loud voice addressing everybody in the darkened room, "we are not safe here."

A woman sitting beside her mother said: "Sh, sh, carefully, Frau Schubert. The children!"

But her mother went on: "We will not survive this if they don't do something for us right now. Why did the sirens come on so late?"

"That's what I was just asking myself," the man from downstairs said, "someone can't have been paying proper attention. The enemy is not that fast."

After a while they could hear the planes leaving. It was when she expected to be brought up again to her bed that men's voices could be heard on the street.

"It's not over. Come out. Quick. We'll accompany you to the shelter," someone shouted and pounded against the bars of the cellar window. Then the man's voice could be heard again. "Come out."

Three soldiers were waiting for them in front of the house.

"You are wonderful," her mother cried in excitement. "I know you. You belong to my husband's company."

The soldiers did not listen. They took her brother and two other small children into their arms, reached for prams and luggage and said again: "We really do have to hurry. They are on their way again."

At this stage she was not afraid of the bombs anymore, although she could hear the sound of planes. She marched as fast as she could. She thought: 'I am a big child. I do not have to be carried.' But when one of the soldiers took her hand she did not protest. For a moment she thought of telling the friendly man that her mother always went with her sister. She could see both of them in front. Then she decided not to talk to him. Her mother was speaking with her loud voice just now anyway. Her mother addressed everybody in their group telling them she had definitely known there would be help. "The Leibstandarte soldiers are the best," she cried. "They know what to do. In all this trouble Hitler is looking after us, the families of his men."

When they reached the air-raid shelter some women she had never seen before with children in their arms approached them in the empty street. They pointed to the air raid shelter and said something. She did not understand what they were saying. Again there was a roaring noise coming from the sky. They all stopped now. The man from downstairs started to talk to the women. But her mother interrupted him. Waving a hand her mother said: "No, no. Not here. This is a Leibstandarte shelter. Go down the road and then left. It's not far. You will be fine there."

It was the first time that she slept in her underground bed. They stayed there all night. When the sirens finally signalled 'All clear' it was already morning. They set off home.

"Look! Our house is still there," her mother cried, "but the curtains!"

Although the adults would think a little girl like her would not know about anything she understood very well that the curtains of the children's room were streaming like a flag out of the window because the glass was broken.

―――

Santa is Coming 1942

"Only three more sleeps left, then Santa is coming," her mother said. "Even though there is war I know for certain he is on his way."

She knew how much three times was. She would be four years old after the winter and had practised a lot with the numbers from one to ten. When you were four you had to know how to count and be able to read the clock. Her sister refused to share her knowledge of mathematics with her. Her mother never had time to answer such questions because of the war. The war had started when she was a tiny baby and still looked like her baby doll. But her grandmother had helped her learn her numbers when she was visiting them. Her grandmother only stayed a few days because her grandmother did not like to be in Berlin and so near to Hitler. Adolf Hitler was the name of the Führer. Her mother was angry with her grandmother for not talking nicely about the Führer. The Führer was a good man, her mother said, and he had given them this nice apartment. And now the Führer was sending his Santa to all the children in the Leibstandarte housing complex. After only three more sleeps.

The time dragged by interminably till the Führer's Santa eventually arrived one morning. Her sister had dressed earlier and ran down the stairs while she still battled with the scarf around her neck and the buttons on her coat. It was bitterly cold outside and the Führer had just sent coal to heat the stove in the sitting room. Her mother said the Führer looked after them because her father looked after the Führer. Her father was one of his special guards and that was a very important job and they all had to be happy.

Santa sat on the back of an open lorry. He waved but drove on. "He is going to stop at the playground," her sister shouted back to the nice girl living in the apartment below them. The nice girl started running and she did too. Santa vanished around the corner. But all the children caught up with him at the playground entrance.

"Don't try to catch them," her sister ordered as Santa's shower of sweets fell upon them, "pick them up and put them into this bag." It was her mother's crochet bag that she had chosen to take with her earlier that morning. But her mother had said: "That's the good one. I don't want it to get dirty. Give it to your sister." Her sister was often allowed to do what she was not. Although she could actually be more careful than her.

The bag was pretty full when Santa left. He had personally put an apple for her little brother at home into the bag. They went on shouting "Happy Christmas," even long after the lorry and Santa, his sack still quite full, were gone.

"He is bringing sweets to all the children in the town. Not only to us!" she proclaimed and in high spirits turned round and round with her arms stretched out wide calling: "Happy Christmas to all of us!"

"Stop that nonsense," her sister addressed her angrily. Her sister was closing the zip on their bag.

"The Jewish children don't get sweets," the nice girl said.

"That's right," her sister nodded in agreement.

She did not want to be told what she was supposed to think. Emphasising her words, she said: "At Christmas all children get sweets. The Jewish ones too."

Her sister looked at her very scornfully and remarked: "Ask mother."

———

A Beautiful Sky 1943

Her little brother had an awful cough and that's why, fortunately, their nanny Ruth travelled with her and her sister to their grandmother's. To the one who lived in Preetz and was called 'Grandma Preetz' because the other grandma was called 'Grandma Kiel'. She had never been in Preetz. Her Grandmother Preetz came every Christmas to tell them the latest about the ghost that lived in Grandma Preetz's attic.

"There is no ghost anymore," her mother, who had accompanied them to the station said while they were waiting for the train. "Grandma Preetz has other worries now. Both her sons are away fighting for our fatherland."

It was difficult to understand that one of Grandma's sons was her father and one her uncle. She knew sons. Women in their housing block had sons. But those sons were boys, as little as she was herself.

Her mother was right. The ghost in the house in Preetz had left before they arrived. He had taken all his belongings with him. So he would not be back soon. But her grandmother had new news to report. Every night they would all be able to watch Christmas trees covered in lights falling from the sky. Of course that was something she could not wait to see. And there was even more to be astonished about. She and her sister would have to go to bed with their full clothes on. And even, she could not believe it, with their boots. Every night.

Ruth was not so non-plussed. Ruth smiled and said: "That's right. You know we have to hurry when the siren starts to wail. Grandma Preetz is afraid she wouldn't be able to dress you quickly enough. Sometimes the bombers arrive before anybody can start the alarm."

She loved her grandmother, although her grandmother had let the ghost go. Her grandmother was able to look into people's hearts. To see if they were good or bad. Her grandmother had learnt it from the blind people she taught when she was young. The blind could not see, it's true, but they could detect something in people's hearts that nobody else would know about. The blind were happy men and women her grandmother said. They only needed help with cooking or walking in an unfamiliar place.

Her grandmother let them have a hot bath after breakfast. They had to undress anyway to put on fresh underwear. Nobody had woken her up the first night. "Maybe the enemy needed a good night's sleep as well," her grandmother said. "But they will definitely fly over Preetz tonight. They know there are new submarines in the Kiel shipyard and they will be determined to destroy them."

Kiel, that was grandmother Kiel's place, she thought. Her grandmother there had to go into her cellar then. She knew the bombs did not always fall where they should. Often they fell on houses where nobody was involved in the war. That's what her mother had said. And that it was not right.

She liked the big bath and splashing water all around and at her sister. Her sister sat up straight opposite her with the usual critical face and soon complained: " I shall tell mother how you've behaved."

She was alarmed. But not for long. Her grandmother appeared in the doorway with an amused look on her face and said to her sister: "That's a good idea, dear. Make sure you don't forget. Your mother will be delighted to hear that you had a good time."

It was actually the following night that the Christmas trees fell from the sky. First there was the alarm, this awful howling sound. She woke up. Then there was Ruth who whispered: "Take your time, little one, they are not after us. We'll stay up here."

Her grandmother led them into the sitting room. Naturally in the dark. She knew from Berlin already that nobody was allowed to let the least bit of light creep out under the blinds. So as not to show the planes were the cities and villages were. Her grandmother had old blinds with holes in them and therefore only lit candles during the night. Candles were not that bright. The blinds were pulled up now.

"They won't drop any bombs around here," her grandmother said . "They need all of them to destroy the ships in Kiel. Now, my girl, you can see why the bombers have to bring their own light to find the submarines."

Yes, there they were, the extraordinary Christmas trees! She was given permission to stand on the windowsill while her sister put a piece of paper onto a chair and stood on that. Ruth had got a letter from her boyfriend in Berlin that day and was in good spirits. She let out lots of different noises of joy and admiration about the beautiful, sparkling sky. The noise from the planes then was just above the house.

"In Berlin they bomb without light," her sister said and sounded as though she was proud of the fact.

"Berlin is better known, even in the dark," her grandmother said.

"It is the capital of the Grossdeutsche Reich," her sister added in the same knowing voice.

The glittering light died. The droning of the bombers faded away. Her grandmother closed the curtains and they went to bed again. She kept her boots on. She had been told that the planes would drop the rest of their bombs here and there on their way home. Without the all clear signal from the siren nobody should relax. But she did. The sky had been so beautiful. And she was sure her grandmother would wake her again if necessary. Her Grandma Preetz was terrific. Yes, she was.

———

On the Tennis Court 1943

She did not like to go to the tennis court of the Leibstandarte. She wasn't meant to be learning to play tennis. Only to wait around there. Her mother was seeing friends and had great fun. That meant her mother and the other women hit the balls and shouted and laughed and applauded each other and her mother got very excited and red in the face. But the other women did not bring their children. She was always on her own. Only sometimes there was a baby sleeping in a pram near the clubhouse. She had to be there because Ruth was busy with the cooking and looking after her little brother. Her sister refused to come and sit about at that boring clay court. Her sister was already big enough to play with the nice girl at the playground.

Her sister was right. It was boring where she was sitting. It was dark and cold under the tall trees. She always asked to be allowed to sit quietly in the sun beside the tennis court. But her mother said the children's place was under the trees between the shrubs in the shade where they could play and enjoy themselves without bothering the adults. But she was four years old now and so too old to make sand-pies and build sand-castles. Ruth, who was the best nanny in the word, said that was true.

The only interesting time was when soldiers came marching from her father's barracks past the tennis court. The soldiers always sang. It seemed to her they sang with such happiness as their feet stamped the ground. She knew all the songs. Her mother sang the lyrics very clearly while cooking or ironing. It was all about fighting and being victorious and following the Führer and the flag waving in front of them. The women stopped playing tennis when soldiers passed by. They even stopped talking, some waved to a husband. They all stared toward the street. They looked moved, especially when one of the songs came to an end in front of them. Then the soldiers bellowed in excitement: ..."for today Germany belongs to us... and tomorrow the whole world."

She sat on a tree trunk beside the sandy court. She felt cold and pulled her jacket closer to her body. Out there where her mother just let out a yell of joy seemed like a different world from where she was. She did not belong to her mother's world.

———

Covering the Star

'Sternverdeckung', covering of the star, was a long word she had learnt and she could say it from the very beginning without breaking off. But her mother wouldn't allow her to say it. Her mother asked where she had heard it. She shrugged. There was something she felt for that man in the shop and did not want to tell her mother. Especially not when her mother had such a critical expression on her face.

When she had been shopping with Ruth there was a queue in the shop. Everyone wanted some of the potatoes that had just come in. Because it was war it was a surprise that there were some extra potatoes. While they waited Ruth talked to a soldier who invited her to a dance. Ruth said no and smiled and pointed at her. But the soldier was not looking at her. At that moment he stepped back and grasped the arm of a man who had winked at her in a friendly way just before.

"What do we have here? Let us see!" the soldier said aloud. Everyone in the shop looked up to see the soldier tugging off the man's enormous scarf which had hung down the front of his coat. The soldier pointed at the big yellow star fixed to the man's chest.

"This is a real case of 'Sternverdeckung', covering the star," the soldier said with the same domineering voice "You come with me! Now!"

Nobody moved. Ruth too stood motionless. Everybody's eyes followed the soldier and the man to the door. The man said, his voice only a whisper: "But I felt so cold today. We have no heating."

The soldier laughed and looked back into the shop asking: "Did you hear that? He was warming his Jewish star."

The man looked back at the crowd as well. She had the impression he was begging for something. Then he looked at her again. And winked. Yes, he did it again. Then the two were gone. The selling of the potatoes went on. Nobody talked about the incident.

At home she asked her mother what "Sternverdeckung" was and said that it sounded great.

"Stop talking like that," her mother answered. That was when she realised how hard it was to work out which questions adults liked and which not. But she could not stop herself saying: "The soldier was not nice to the man."

"He was a Jew. Ruth told me." Her mother retreated into the kitchen and made herself busy at the sink.

"And a Jew is bad?" She felt the urgent need for an answer.

"Yes he is. All of them are." Her mother turned and looked her in the eye. She saw clearly that her mother was disturbed by her questions. Now she regretted having said Sternverdeckung to her mother at all. She felt dreadful when her mother looked at her like this. She always had a sense of failure.

She thought it better to leave her mother alone. As she was leaving the kitchen to see if she could get some attention from Ruth, her mother shouted behind her: "The only thing the Jews want is to harm the German Reich. We won't allow that."

Later she tried the nice sounding word again. Secretly. The man did have such a loving look.

In the Tram 1943

After the friendly man had winked at her she hoped to meet him again. Sometimes they met a person with a big yellow star on their chest. Then she looked into the person's face to see if she could find the friendly eyes. But they did not meet Jews in the wide streets. Only in narrow ones away from shopping areas. "There are only a few Jews left , thank God," her mother said to Ruth one day, "here in Berlin the evacuation will soon be over."

She did not know what all that meant and asked her sister. Her sister always knew everything even though she didn't go to school yet either. But even her sister had to ask.

"The Jews are sent away to live in their own community," her mother explained in a low voice to her sister. "Berlin will be free of Jews in a short while. Like Vienna. Baldur von Schirach is doing a good job there."

Her mother often mentioned that man with the curious name and said that he had looked after the youth of the Reich so well. Her mother really seemed to admire him.

One day in a tram she thought she had found the friendly man. But then she realised it was not him. His hair was different. It was white. But the man and she looked at each other. Sitting in the front of the tram beside her sister and Ruth, with her mother and her little brother behind them, she had turned back by accident and noticed the star. The tram was swaying a lot and the man with the star was holding on to a pole so as not to fall. She wondered why he was not sitting down. She could see several empty seats in the tram.

She looked at her sister and asked: "Why is that man standing? That one with the star? He should sit down. He is old enough to be a grandfather."

Her sister looked back, turned forward again and answered with an arrogant air: "He is not allowed to."

"Why?" she asked.

"Shut up," her sister said.

"Why?" she insisted.

Her sister shook her head. But her mother asked from behind: "What's going on?"

Her sister made a throwaway gesture with her hand and reported behind: "Her stupid ideas."

"Tell me," her mother said. But her sister was reluctant and shook her head.

"Tell me," her mother repeated.

Just then the tram went round a bend and tilted to one side. She looked back to the Jewish man. He was holding on to the pole, now with both hands.

"I want a star myself," she said very audibly and waited eagerly for a response from someone. She noticed some people looked first at her and then at her mother.

"Stop that," her sister said. But she could not stop herself.

"I want a star for myself," she demanded in the same loud voice.

Just then the tram stopped. Two women entered through the front door and took a seat. The tram started again.

"Hold on!" A man who was sitting in front of her got up and addressed the tram driver: "Hold on a minute. I shall settle this."

The man smoothed his hands over his uniform jacket,

looked around so as to get attention and then went to the back of the tram. "Out!" he commanded in a frightening voice as he approached the man with the star. "I am saying 'Out'. Your lot can walk!"

She had got up too and was now kneeling on her seat looking backwards. She saw the man jumping out of the back door and struggling not to fall. The man in the uniform laughed. He took his seat again. Some people also laughed. Some did not look up. The tram went on.

"Sit down!" her mother said. Her mother had not moved the whole time. For a while she did not hear a word from behind her. Then her mother started talking to Ruth about what to cook for dinner that day.

———

Ruth is not Working 1943

When it was her fourth birthday she had not had a party. Her mother had said there were too many air raids in Berlin. Mostly at night. Everybody had to look for a safe place in the cellars of their houses or in air raid shelters. People slept in the daytime or queued for bread and butter and had no time to congratulate a little girl on now being almost as sensible as her sister. There was no chocolate either. She had been looking forward to getting some, the kind in the round tin that she liked so much. But her mother did not get any. There was hardly anything available. You couldn't even buy a saucepan. Her sister knew that the material a saucepan was made from was badly needed to make weapons.

On the day before her birthday her mother had got a letter from her father in Russia. Her father, who was in the Waffen SS now, had sent congratulations. To the adults he wrote that their final victory in the war was close now because they had got thousands of new soldiers in the Waffen SS. "The Germans are taking revenge for stalingrit now," her mother said.

She did not know what revenge was, nor 'stalingrit.' Only that it had made many brave German soldiers die in freezing weather. Her mother had explained that to have a birthday party at this hard time would be wrong. Herr Hitler did not want them to squander time and goods that were so important for the war.

For a while she had been disappointed about the failure of her big day. But then, later in spring, there was more bad news. Ruth was to leave them to work in a factory. Her nanny was needed to build bullets and bombs that would be directed against the aggressors.

Her mother was completely distraught about this letter. "I cannot raise three children and keep the house without help," her mother cried.

"I know," Ruth said.

Her grandmother from Kiel, who had come to stay for a few days, smiled wryly: "I had three myself dear, an apartment without a bathroom, no help and my husband came home for dinner every day and I am still alive."

"But not in such terrible times." Her mother sounded enraged.

"The First World War, which the Germans also started, was no easier than yours is now." Her grandmother kept smiling.

"Stop it! Please," her mother shouted.

"I would prefer to stay," Ruth said. Ruth was still only a girl herself. "But you said we all have to give up our private wishes for Hitler and..."

"You are right." Her mother's expression changed and stopped being so frightening. In a calmer voice her mother went on: "I shall pull myself together now. The boys out there at the front suffer more than we do here. We lonely mothers have to let them know that we can manage. That will give them strength. And you...," her mother was now looking at her and her little brother..., "you go and play. You shouldn't listen to adults' conversations."

Ruth stayed with them. Her mother went to work as a secretary in the barracks of the Leibstandarte instead.

Life changed. Her mother seemed very happy about the new arrangement. Every morning, while her mother was dressing as if for a Sunday outing, Ruth made the breakfast for all of them, then did the dishes, dressed her little brother, cleaned the house and soaked a lot of washing in the bath. Ruth had some new, different ideas about how they might play with their toys in the sitting room while she did the ironing and then made lunch, all the while singing all the songs she still knew from her own childhood. In the afternoon they went for a walk or amused themselves in the playground of the Leibstandarte complex. But then Ruth had so much to get ready for her mother's return that it got boring in their apartment and she missed her mother. Even if her mother never took any notice of her.

One day Ruth took them to meet her mother at the barracks after work. They had to wait a long time till her mother appeared. Her mother was wearing a costume that Ruth had ironed the night before. She thought her mother looked beautiful with her red curled hair and her slim figure. But her mother did not meet them straight away. There was a soldier with a rifle standing in a wooden hut beside the barracks entrance. Her mother smiled at the soldier and said something to him in a friendly manner. Her mother looked very happy and showed no sign of tiredness. The soldier did not move nor could she hear him answering. By then her sister had reached her mother and got a hug. Her mother took her sister's hand and walked toward her and Ruth and her brother, now with a face that had lost the aroused, open look of a moment earlier.

Her mother said: "Hello there, Ruth. Let's go. I had a hard day. Thank god I am so quick at the typewriter and they value it, these men." Her mother went on with her sister.

She would have liked to hold her mother's hand too. But her mother did not offer it and anyway was already walking several steps in front of her. Her little brother in Ruth's arms shouted: "I got a red pencil! I drew a clown." Her mother answered "Great!" without looking back.

They went home in a group of two and three. The dinner Ruth had cooked only needed to be warmed up.

At bedtime her sister asked her mother for a story.

"I am tired. Sorry dear," her mother answered. "Ask Ruth."

"She will be too tired as well," her sister supposed.

Her mother looked up with wide eyes. "How come? Ruth is not working."

———

Poland 1943

There was an air raid almost every night. As soon as they heard the sirens wailing they had to grab a few things and hurry to the air raid shelter. One morning her mother told her and her sister to pack. Soon they would be leaving for Posen. There would be a lorry to take their beds and a bus to take them and their suitcases. They were leaving because more and more bombs were being dropped on Berlin. And her mother and all the other women feared for the safety of their dear children.

The next night in the shelter the women were talking more than usual. She could not sleep despite being told to by her mother, and she heard that Posen was a place on the river Warthe. All the Leibstandarte families would live in a big manor house which was chosen especially for them by the SS. They would wait there till the terrible war was over. That would be soon. The women knew there were a lot of German soldiers in Posen to make sure everything went right there. When she heard this she began to hope her father would be there as well so her mother would not be so restless anymore.

It was a long journey to Posen. Her little brother cried most of time in Ruth's arms. Her sister talked with her mother. She looked out of the window. She liked the trees and the meadows and the coloured gardens and all the small houses they passed. She wondered what a manor house was like and if their beds had arrived in time.

In fact their beds were already made up when they got there. They were welcomed by two girls on the broad staircase of the large house. One of the girls told them that their family room was on the right-hand side of the hall and that dinner was ready for all the families in the dining room on the left. That girl spoke with a funny accent, the second girl did not speak at all. Then all of a sudden there was running and shouting in the house. The mothers were running up and down and complaining about things that were missing and about the dreadful overcrowding in their rooms. And that they had not brought enough things with them to be able to live a proper life in this awful country. What her mother really missed was a private sitting room and she told Ruth nervously that they definitely would not stay long. She said it was all a bit too much to bear.

"Yes, it is awful here" her sister said, "I don't want to start school in this village. Did you see how the children on the market place were dressed?"

She knew that her sister liked nice, completely clean clothes and had already discovered that there was only one bathroom for all of them.

"At least we are safe here, Frau Schubert," Ruth said, and added that she had just heard the bell to call them to the dining room.

"How do you know that's what it means?" her mother asked.

"The girl told me when we arrived."

"Don't talk to them," her mother commanded. "That's not proper for us."

The girls who had welcomed them had cooked them a fine dinner. The first girl said they were going to do that every day and would prepare the breakfast as well. And that they were employed to do all the washing in the washhouse.

"We will be fine," Ruth said. But her mother was not content. After the meal her mother grasped the arm of the girl who had welcomed them and held her back.

"That other girl is your sister, isn't she?" her mother asked. "Why does she never speak?"

"She does not have your language. We are Polish," the girl replied, "I have picked up a bit of German."

"Where are you living?" her mother went on in her most imperious manner. She did not like the way her mother addressed this girl. It was frightening.

"We used to live here in this house." The girl did not seem afraid.

"And now?"

The girl freed herself from her mother's grip and pointed through one of the back windows into the garden. "Over there. We moved last week."

"It is the servants' house," her mother explained to Ruth when they were back in the room where they would all sleep. "They are fine out there. I just wonder how the family could afford to build such a big house. Poles are not hard working and don't know anything about managing money. But all that will change now that we are here."

Ruth did not answer. Her sister asked: "We?"

"The Germans." Her mother sounded astonished.

She did not sleep well that night although there were no alarms and no planes came and no bombs fell. And fresh air reached her bed through a wide-open window. She had a lot of thinking to do. She did not know what was going on.

In the Big House **1943**

Life in the big house was not as nice as she had hoped when they left Berlin. Their room was full of beds and so she had no room to build farmyards and villages with her brother's toys while Ruth read stories to him. Her sister practised writing words sitting at a coffee table. Her sister was starting school soon and wanted to be top of the class right from the very beginning. Her mother was very excited about that and often said 'Good girl'. But only to her sister.

She played with some of the children from their group in front of the house or in the big hall when it was raining. But the indoor playing was soon stopped. Some of the women did not like the noise at their door, others shrugged, one said children needed room to entertain themselves and one wanted them to go back into their rooms straightaway. Her mother came and exclaimed sharply: "No-one is allowed to order my children about."

They went swimming in a nearby pond. Her mother and the three of them. There were a lot of midges and she had to stay in the water all the time. Her little brother got a lot of bites and her mother cried: "Oh, I have to get out of here."

The school thing almost went wrong. They couldn't find a satchel to buy. Some of the women had brought satchels with them. They had known the Poles would not have satchels. Her mother was too agitated about this to go swimming with them and sent Ruth instead. Although she should have been doing the ironing. "You can do that later tonight," her mother said, "young girls like you can't go out here anyway."

Her mother soon felt better. And she felt better then too. Her mother had found a man who could make satchels and had told him that her wonderful daughter was not to be at a disadvantage among the other girls. Ruth explained to her the word 'disadvantage'. She thought yes, being left out was not nice.

But it was not only the satchel that was not available. Her sister needed a slate to write on and a pencil and, most important, a Zuckertüte, a big bag of sweets. Every child starting school needed a big bag full of sweets and apples and other treats. So that they would be happy and not cry.

Her mother made up the nicest sweet-bag anyone had ever seen and sent one of the Polish girls to the shop to buy things to put in it.

"But there is nothing there," the girl said shaking her head vigorously.

"You tell them it's for the Leibstandarte families," her mother answered unimpressed. "They will know very well."

The girls brought biscuits and nuts and some home-made lollipops. Her mother made a second sweet-bag for a girl who was there without her family and was very proud of herself by the time they all went to bed. "That's me," her mother said, "I can set to at the drop of a hat and I'm always ready to use my talents to help others. I made that little girl very happy."

The next day as the women set off with the children who were starting school, her mother took a photo of her sister with her canvas satchel on her back and the Zuckertüte in her arms. Then the two of them ran off in good spirits to catch up with the rest of the group. Ruth stayed with her and her brother whereas most of the mothers had taken their other children with them as well. "You better stay here," her mother had said the night before, "tomorrow is my eldest daughter's day."

She had hoped her mother would change her mind and take her. But her mother did not. Instead, Ruth took her and her brother to the pond and pointed out how happy they were to have the water totally to themselves. But they had to try hard to enjoy the bathing. She knew for certain Ruth would have liked to go to the school house too. To be nice to Ruth while Ruth was handing her the towel, she said: "When I start school I would like to have a leather satchel like the girl from the second floor. I won't need sweets. But you definitely have to come."

Now Ruth's smile was genuine.

———

Her mother wen...
like living in the big hou...
happy to be there. It was ...
German soldiers were in Russ...
harm from that side. But her m...
and she was dissatisfied with the ...
"No respect," her mother said. And: ...oles'
way of life. They will never achieve a...

She never discovered what her ... ...r wanted the girls to do. She liked the girls. And their mother. She had been secretly visiting their small house. One afternoon when her mother and Ruth took a nap one of the girls had taken her home. Her sister had been busy writing and her little brother was sleeping too. The girl looked around and listened to the sound of the house and then suddenly took her hand and said: "Come on. Say hello to my mother. She wants to get to know you."

The mother made cocoa and offered her a piece of a wonderful fruitcake. Then she learned that the father had disappeared on the very day before she and all the others from the Leibstandarten complex had arrived.

The girl looked at her mother and said in a pleading tone: "Please!"

"He will come back after the war. I know that," the mother answered and picked up the pot of cocoa. Some of the cocoa poured out over the beautiful table cloth. But it did not matter. The mother got a fresh one and after a while the girl brought her back to the big house. She knew she must not tell

said: "If someone asks tell them
hens."

_ any questions. No one was interested in
_he time. Her mother wanted to leave as soon as
_d one long morning wrote a letter to her father at the
_ about the awful, good-for-nothing life in Poland.

Soon afterwards they got a response from her father and again there was excitement and packing. Her father had chosen a new place for his family to live, her mother said. Because he was very important he always had people at his command. Her mother could not bring their beds but her father had sent someone to Berlin to pack up all their other furniture and send it to Austria. That's where they were going to live. They would have a wonderful house at the Woerthersee, her mother said, on the beautiful lake itself and they would look out at the Karawanken mountains. After that, they would only move once more, when the war was over. Her father had written that he planned to live in England, which would then belong to Germany.

While they were in the train to Austria she thought about where England was. And if she would like to stay there. Would she be able to go to school with no English? Without the language she would be as dumb as the second Polish girl. And what if she liked the mountains and the lake so much and did not want to go to England at all? That was where the bombers came from. And would her mother like the people? Would the English do everything the right way? The way her mother wanted?

———

Arriving in Pörtschach **1943**

Her sister, her little brother and she all suffered from diarrhoea during the endless journey to Pörtschach. Her mother said it was the worst journey she had ever made. In a dirty, overcrowded train with three sick children through a country shaken by war. Ruth kept smiling and said: "There hasn't been a single air raid to stop us. And we do know where we are going."

She liked to hear Ruth speaking in a calm voice. And she liked sitting beside Ruth. She felt safe then. Ruth went on addressing her mother: "It's summer, Frau Schubert. We are not cold. And we have plenty of food. I wonder where the girls got it for us."

"The cheese is for us children," her sister insisted.

"No! It is just for me!" The moment she said this she regretted it. But she missed the girl who was so nice and had trusted her.

"I know she liked you," her mother said, "but she should not have favoured you."

In Pörtschach the mayor was waiting for them at the station. Her mother had telegraphed the mayor to say that the wife of a Waffen SS officer was coming with her three children to be the guests of the Gauleiter in his guesthouse by the lake. "It will be his duty to receive us," her mother had said earlier .

The mayor was very friendly. He brought two cars and one chauffeur and drove them to the opposite shore of the lake. The village there had a funny name: Maria Woerth. She slept in a room that was painted light blue with fine white embroidered curtains and she had a snow white blanket and two cushions. She woke up to see the sunbeams dancing on the water just in front of the window. She sat up. She was happy. She felt safe and thought she must be in a different world all of a sudden.

Then her sister announced: "I am going to see the school today. Mother is bringing me and will show me Pörtschach as well. And we are going to visit the family of Herr Meyer, the teacher. He is father's friend and in the Waffen SS too and knows the Gauleiter very well." Her sister sounded very proud and after a pause jumped out of bed saying: "At school they will have to respect me."

"Can I come?" she asked with little hope.

"Certainly not." Her sister gave her little brother a light slap to wake him. "I'm telling you, mother needs a break from her little ones. Ruth will look after you."

———

In the Guesthouse 1943

She really loved the Gauleiter's house. It was called Karinderhütte. She loved every day they spent there. It was summer. It was warm. They could bathe in the lake and her mother could show all of them how easy swimming was. Her mother could swim very well. And her mother could sail too, she was told. She wanted to learn to swim immediately. But her sister had to have lessons first.

Lunch and dinner were served in a blue house beside the Karinderhütte. They had plenty to eat and there were never any air raids. The only planes she saw were the Fiseler Storch ones.

"German planes," her mother said, "on their way to Italy."

The Fiseler Storchs were small planes. You could hear them coming by the sound of the propeller. One afternoon, when they were sitting on the terrace in beautiful painted chairs with real coffee and a cake that the woman who washed their clothes had baked, a 'Fiseler Storch' came flying low over their heads. She could see the pilot with his big glasses.

Her mother jumped to her feet. "Come on, Ruth," her mother ordered, "clear the plates away."

Ruth looked bewildered but put the cups onto the ground and then the plates and the coffee pot while her mother was pulling at one end of the table cloth. The table cloth came off and soon it was waving in the air like a flag. Her mother looked up at the little plane with great delight all over her face while with both hands she worked hard to keep the cloth moving.

"He has noticed us," her mother cried, "can you see how

he is looking down?"

The cloth kept waving while the plane flew away from them. She was just hoping they would all sit down again and have more cake when her mother cried out again. "Look! He is waving as well. He is answering me. Wonderful. The plane is dipping its wings! He must know we are Germans too."

Reluctantly she looked up. Yes, her mother was right. The plane was swinging from one side to the other. Again and again.

"They are great, these pilots," her mother called out, still very excited. "How lucky we are to have such brave men. Africa is lost, but we will keep Italy."

She did not know what Africa was, or Italy. The names sounded funny. She asked aloud without hesitating. And she looked at her mother who was still following the plane with her eyes. Then the plane disappeared in a gap between the mountains. Her mother must have heard her question but did not answer as she sat down again.

Her sister looked at her with furrows in her brow and said: "Be quiet. You are too small to understand." She noticed her mother was smiling at her sister. "Don't bother mother."

Before she could think of anything to defend herself Ruth took her hand. "Let's see if the water is nice and warm for some splashing around. We'll have some fun. Who wants to come?"

Only her brother wanted to come. The water was fine and to her surprise Ruth could swim. Ruth had never shown them before. That day she learnt how to move her arms and legs to keep her body on top of the water. She decided to become a good swimmer and next summer she would swim across the

Woerthersee. If only she could see Grandmother Preetz and ask why the thing called Africa was lost and who Italy was.

———

Villa Caprice 1943

Several days later her mother and sister came back from Pörtschach and met Ruth, her brother and herself on the private beach belonging to the Karinderhütte. Her mother looked happy and soon started to report: "We are going to live in a marvellous house. Just over there." Her mother pointed to the opposite shore of the lake. "The Gauleiter let me choose a house. Imagine, I could pick whatever I wanted and it would be freed for us. I must say I think I've made a good choice. And nobody has to move out for us. The house I chose is empty. Some of the time empty, I should say."

Her mother sat down and smoothed out her skirt. Then went on in her excited voice: "We will have a boat house with a nice old fashioned boat in it and there is an island with a little bridge and a second long one beside the boathouse to go swimming from. We will have a wonderful life there till the war is over. I am so looking forward to seeing our furniture arrive and to moving in."

She was not looking forward to this. She really loved it in the Karinderhütte .

"Who owns the house?" Ruth asked.

"People in Klagenfurt. They use it as a Bed and Breakfast."

"They will lose their business then," Ruth said.

"In these hard times people lose more than their business," her mother told Ruth. "I had to leave the home I loved so much and I am here without any of my belongings."

Now her sister raised a finger and pointed at her mother:

"You just said the furniture will be coming."

"It is," her mother answered with a heavy sigh," but it will take time for the soldiers to pack everything and it will take time till it arrives. Trains are slow now. And it is a long way from Berlin to Austria."

Ruth did not say anything. Ruth packed their towels and swimsuits together. Her mother went on wailing: "I am longing for a bit of peace. I am burnt out. We have been on the move for three months. Life is hard for a mother in war times. Even for mothers wearing a Mothercross."

She was taken by surprise when on one of the following mornings her mother let her come with them to her sister's school. They crossed the lake in a steam boat and after letting her sister off her mother walked with her through Pörtschach and further on. They passed fields and orchards. The railway tracks ran near the road on the left. She could spot the lake sometimes through the hedges and bushes which surrounded some houses on her right hand side. Eventually her mother stopped and pointed down a driveway saying: "There we are. That's the Villa Caprice. Isn't it wonderful?"

Yes, it was, she thought. But did not say it. She was still confused. Why had her mother brought her? Only her? And why was her mother talking to her in such a caring voice? Her mother never did that .

"Do you like it? Tell me!"

She looked at her mother and then at the house again. There was a wooden balcony running along the side of the house with a wrought iron railing with lots of hearts in it. To the left she saw tall trees and glittering water behind them. To the right there was a second house, a tiny one. Two boys were playing in front of it. She looked at the boys and all of a sudden felt a strong impulse to say hello to them.

"They're of no interest to us," her mother said also looking at the boys. "They are Austrians. Their mother used to look after the villa. But we are here now."

"Will they play with me?" She could not stop herself asking that.

"Look, there is the pump where we get our water. Things aren't modern here. But it will do as long as the war lasts."

They were still standing at the gate. She glimpsed a boat in the middle of the lake. "Are we staying here?" The boys were staring at them now.

"Oh, yes."

"How long?" One of the boys waved at her. She moved her right hand sideways slowly up and down so that her mother could not see it.

"As I said till the war is..."

"Why is there a war?" she heard herself asking and was highly surprised that she dared to asked such a question. Now her mother would say: You don't understand. But she knew a war was when the fathers were at the front and there were enemies who shot the soldiers and bombed houses and ships. But why did they do it?

"The Jews are to blame for that," her mother answered in the tone that indicated anger. "They are everywhere and they only ever look after their own welfare."

Her mother spoke the word 'their' extra loudly. "They are the trouble-makers in the world."

Her mother seemed to get upset about the Jews so she tried to change the subject and asked very politely: "Can we go to the house now?"

They went down the drive. Her mother nodded at the boys but did not stop to talk to them. She would have liked to know their names. So that she would know something that her sister didn't. But her mother took her to the front of the house and looked at the roses. Then suddenly she turned and declared: "Let's go. I have to get the keys. They should have handed them over to me already. Because the house is ours now."

Her mother had to wait a few days for the keys and told Ruth the Austrians were almost as useless as the Polish. When a man finally brought the keys her mother took her sister to the Villa. Ruth had wanted to see the house as well but was not taken. She felt sorry for Ruth and suggested going to pick blueberries. It was boring picking blueberries but Ruth liked it and was always happy doing it.

———

Grandmother 1943-44

"You go and play," her mother ordered every morning after her sister had left for school, "you have got everything children could wish for here in this paradise." But she and her brother had nothing to play with.

Her mother was happy in the new house and told Frau Gruber in the gate lodge that life was enjoyable again. Frau Gruber was working hard all day cutting wood and growing vegetables and making clothes for her children. There was no Herr Gruber to help her carry the water into the house. Frau Gruber was nice and so were her two boys. In the afternoon they played with her and let her come into their house to have some milk.

Once she invited them to her house but her mother made them leave again. Her sister's teacher was coming to help her sister to catch up at school so that she could move into the second class in the autumn even though she had been in the first for only a few months. From this she deduced that it would be two years before she got any of the attention her sister now received. Then she would go to school as well and meet other children.

On her fifth birthday her mother surprised her by announcing that her Grandmother Kiel was coming to stay with them for as long as the Allies were still bombing the towns in Germany. The army was going to stop them doing that soon, her mother explained, and the army would also stop the Russians who were in any case only making progress at a snail's pace. Her mother had read this in the newspapers and was no longer worried about her father who was away with his comrades fighting the Russians.

She looked forward to her grandmother's arrival. It would be spring then, the summer would come and the water would be warm enough for swimming. She wondered if her grandmother could swim and would come in the water with her. She felt lonely sometimes and Grandmother Kiel would be someone to lean on. She never left the grounds of the Villa. Her mother did the shopping on her bicycle or went to see the wife of Herr Mayer, the teacher, to get news about the Waffen SS. Ruth was busy with washing and cooking all day and only left the house sometimes in the evening to meet a friend.

Her grandmother got an extra piece of meat at her first dinner in Pörtschach. "People in Kiel live on turnips and water," her grandmother reported, "and they freeze." She learnt that the houses on both sides of her grandmother's apartment house had been bombed and burnt out. Her grandmother's apartment and the others in her block were all right because everybody who had been there that night had given a hand to get water and save the building. And they even had plenty of light to do the job by because the flames had illuminated the scene so well.

"We are fine here," her mother said, not asking if her grandmother had been hurt or where the children who lived in her grandmother's apartment house had been that night. "The Gauleiter is looking after us very well." Her mother's voice had a note of pride in it. "He does it so that our men out there know that their families are fine. That will help them fight."

She noticed a slight smile on her grandmother's face. And a barely discernible shaking of the head as her grandmother answered: "My neighbours don't have a Gauleiter to make them comfortable. They are happy if they survive the day. The families in the towns where the Nazis build their weapons and ships suffer most. Hitler will have to make an end to this madness soon."

Suddenly, when her grandmother had finished talking about the war in Kiel, her mother's face turned a deep red and she jumped up and ran out of the room. The door shut with a loud bang, but opened again and they could hear her mother's voice: "Don't you know it is dangerous to say such things? Talk like that undermines the morale of our troops and you can be punished for it. I am warning you."

Her grandmother now actually smiled as she answered: "You had me come here so you could look after me. But I see the great German Reich comes first!" Her grandmother raised an arm and held it out sideways like people in the newspapers always did and, sounding like the Führer on the radio, proclaimed: "Sacrifices have to be made for the final victory!"

This time her mother slammed the door even louder. She tried not to forget the word 'sacrifices' to ask her grandmother about it later. Her grandmother kept smiling and said: "My dear children, these times are hard for all of us. Let's go for a walk and look to see if there are any wild strawberries yet. If we find some we can make pancakes with them afterwards. I am not too proud to use Herr Gauleiter's flour and eggs."

———

Soldiers' Songs **1944**

Sometimes her mother was in a good mood. After they had been in the lake one day and she had been jumping from the bridge and then crawling back through the water to the steps at the end of the bridge, her mother came and sat down with them on a patch of grass in the sunshine. Her sister started to recite poems that they were taught at school. One of them her sister spoke with a heavy Kaernten accent. It sounded very funny. Her little brother laughed. Her sister seemed to like her role as entertainer and repeated the words. The poem said: "Germans we are, German we'll remain, because Germany is the ground on which we grow and shall go on growing."

"Wonderful," her mother exclaimed, "but please, dear, don't pick up the Austrian accent too much. As you said, we are Germans after all."

Her mother was wearing blue trousers and a white bikini top. She thought her mother was a beautiful woman. Others liked her mother as well. Her mother often said that things could never go wrong if an attractive, clever woman was involved. "I know I am liked," her mother once said, "I have a nature that everyone warms to."

To her surprise her mother stayed with them for a while that day. Her brother wanted to sing the Horst Wessel song. She knew all the words from the tennis court but did not know who Horst Wessel was. Her mother said he had made up this great song and Hitler chose it as his favourite. Her mother sang in a loud voice: "Die Fahne hoch, die Reihen fest geschlossen!"

When it came to the end of the song her mother's eyes looked very soft. The end seemed to be a promise. It said that tomorrow the whole world would belong to Germany.

"But it will take longer." Her mother sighed and got up, "until then you have to behave very well."

She wanted her mother to stay. "Please can you sing Weißt du wieviel Sterne stehen?"

"That baby song," her sister cried. "No!"

Her mother went into the house. Her sister followed her mother. Her little brother tried to catch up with them. She went to the boathouse and sat down at the far end of the decking. The wind was ruffling the surface of the water. The sun threw tiny glittering lights on the top of the waves. It looked like the picture of the little stars song she had in her head. In the song God was counting all his little stars so as not to lose any of them. She wished she could sing. Then she could hear the song whenever she liked.

The little star song was so different. It had no soldiers in it, no marching or celebrating weapons. This song spoke about God. That he was looking after everyone. Her mother said that was what Hitler was doing. But how could he? He was living with his officers in Berlin or somewhere. Not like God up there looking down at the world.

———

20th July **1944**

"Hitler is dead!" Her mother came home from the shop in Pörtschach and dropped down on a chair in the kitchen, her eyes full of tears. Ruth was just ironing the washing from the last few days, her grandmother was playing cards with her little brother and her sister was doing her homework at the table with a hand held over her notebook so that nobody could see what she was writing. She herself was doing nothing. She had been swimming, but it was too hot outside to stay on the bridge. Until her mother came nobody had spoken because her sister needed silence to do her work. She thought her sister could have had the empty dining room as a study but her mother said her sister was allowed to choose where to study.

"Did you hear me? I said Hitler is dead." Her mother sounded almost angry. "Doesn't anybody have anything to say to such dreadful news?"

Being dead meant gone for ever. That was what she had learnt since the bombs started to fall on Berlin. Death came in the towns and at the front. Her grandmother had told her that the English and Russians got shot and bombed too and that they missed their loved ones just as much as the Germans did theirs. But now this was new. Hitler was dead. So there was no Führer anymore. Would there be no war either? Her mother always said the Führer was needed for the war. She suddenly felt very proud to be asking herself such a clever question.

"What happened?" her grandmother asked, holding her cards.

"Some devil has killed him! The woman in the shop didn't know any more." Her mother took a handkerchief and blew her nose, looked at everybody in the kitchen and after a while went on: "The worst of it was that the Austrians smiled at me. Imagine! The news is the Führer has died and they smile! While I start to cry! Nobody seemed to be sorry. If only I knew more."

"Switch on the radio!" Her sister looked up as she said this, then went on writing.

Her mother's face twisted into a smile as she answered: "I shall. Thank you, dear. Everything is lost now. How are we going to win the war? Just now, when the new miracle weapon is on its way?"

"Would you ever please wake up, daughter." Her grandmother spoke as she dealt out cards to her brother and added: "The war is lost. You should know that! The Allies, thank God, are making good progress and in any case the Russians are practically on our doorstep."

So she was finally going to see a Russian from the country where her father was at the front. But her father was there to make them stay, wasn't he? Oh, it was very complicated and her grandmother would have a few questions to answer tonight.

"Stop talking like that," her mother said addressing her grandmother. Turning to Ruth she asked: "Are you making coffee now? I need some in my state."

"My state is good," her grandmother reported, emphasizing the 'my'. "He is dead, I can go home. I'll take the first train. Thanks for having me here so long."

She hoped her grandmother was joking. A real fear crept up in her. She did not want to be without her grandmother. Or would they move straight to England?

Before her mother switched on the radio the boys from the gate lodge brought news. Hitler was going to talk to his people tonight.

"So he is not dead," Ruth said, " Heinrich is not coming home."

She felt so confused that she had to sit on her bed. Hitler was alive. Ruth's fiancée could not come back. Ruth was clearly sad about it. But if Hitler was not dead her grandmother would stay. And there was something that nobody in the kitchen had mentioned. Her father would not come home either.

She decided to listen carefully at the dining table this evening. Her sister would ask some questions. Her sister was allowed to speak and to ask anything. Her mother would answer in detail with words children could understand. She would find out then if Hitler was dead or not and whether it was good or bad.

———

Horses 1944

A few weeks later her mother lost Paris. The enemy took it. Her mother cried a lot. Because her father had been there with his comrades and her mother as well and had liked it so much. She remembered the time when her mother had been away and Ruth had looked after them. Her mother had had a passport with a nice photo in it and in the passport it said that her mother was a helper of the troops now. Helpers of the troops were allowed to travel.

Her mother liked to talk about the stay in France. They had lived in a villa. A much bigger and nicer one than the Villa Caprice. And her mother had had the best time of her life in Paris. With so much attention from the soldiers and plenty to eat and being there without her children, free to walk to all the shops and make friends with some French people, even though that was technically forbidden. The only thing to displease her mother was when she lived in the house that belonged to a man with snow-white hair and a very expensive suit. That was where she had seen the SS-men putting their dirty boots up on the polished coffee table when they sat by the fire in the hall. The man himself did not live with them in the house and her mother had seen him once standing under a tree outside the fence of the huge garden and looking in at the house. But the man did not come to visit her mother although her mother would have liked that very much.

ˑIt was on the day her sister was running around clamouring for help to get things ready for the beginning of the new school year that a letter arrived from Russia or somewhere. In it her father reported that he was well and that everyone out there in the war was doing well too. Then her father made an exciting announcement; he was sending his personal assistant, that was Heinrich, to Pörtschach to bring two horses. Later she learned that her father was sending these horses because they were now his and he was looking forward to riding them after the war.

"Your father loves horses," her mother said, "he got riding lessons as soon as he joined the Leibstandarte. He must be a pretty good rider by now."

"Heinrich loves horses as well," Ruth said, "he told me a lot about his father's farm. He often sat on a big black horse while it was pulling the plough." Ruth was smiling but had tears in her eyes too, she noticed.

She was happy that Heinrich was coming. And two horses. She would be six in month or so and felt she was well able to try riding. But where to keep the horses?

"We need two stables," she said very audibly and looked at her mother who was still reading the letter.

"Heinrich has to sort all that out." Her mother folded up the letter.

"We should find a place for them now," Ruth remarked. "They will be tired after the journey from Russia to Kaernten."

"Ask someone at Werners' farm." Her mother made to leave the kitchen.

"Did father send greetings to all of us?" her sister asked.

"Oh, yes." Her mother unfolded the letter. "Didn't I read it to you? Let me see. So, here, after the kisses for myself, he says: "Tell our eldest to be brave and hug the little ones for me.""

She tried to imagine what her father looked like. But she could not form a picture in her head. Nowhere in the house was there a photo of her father. Her mother kept one in her handbag but seldom showed it. She liked it, her father with his officer's cap. Only there was a shadow on his face. From the tank just behind him, her mother had said.

In the evening it was all sorted out. The people at Werners' farm where they sometimes got vegetables were happy to take the horses as soon as they arrived. The Werners did not have horses to work with anymore. The war had taken them away and the loss had made the work on the farm very hard.

"They were so happy," her mother said when she got back from the farm, "they thanked me so much and will give us some potatoes. If the horses are young they will break them in or train them with a cart if they have only ever been ridden."

Ruth looked at her mother for a while and then, in a low voice, asked: "Did your husband say when Heinrich will arrive?"

Her mother shook her head and furrows appeared between her eyes. "You wait and see. I spoke to the stationmaster. He said trains are never punctual now. And trains carrying goods are held up everywhere. A lot of tracks are blocked. There has been sabotage as well. How can anyone…"

"Shouldn't refugees be in the train instead of horses?" her grandmother asked, "I imagine a lot of people are in trouble in the east with the Russians making so much progress."

"Please keep your opinion to yourself," her mother answered, looking very annoyed, "the only progress they are making is at a snail's pace and the Führer still has some trumps in his hand."

She knew what trumps were. Her grandmother

sometimes let her little brother have some when they played cards. To have trumps meant people would look at you and applaud and you would get points. So, Hitler must be happy, she thought. That would make her mother happy too. Maybe her mother would sing with them at bedtime. But her mother would have to be very happy for that.

———

Riding 1944

To everyone's surprise they didn't have to wait long for Heinrich and the horses.

"We had right-of-way everywhere," Heinrich said with a laugh. Heinrich laughed a lot. She noticed Ruth looked different and smiled almost all the time. Heinrich and Ruth kissed everywhere.

Heinrich laughed when she and her sister found them embracing in the kitchen one day. "I am lucky," he said looking at her, "and I'll tell you why. Your father, the Sturmbannführer, had to stay and keep the enemy at bay. I was allowed to take a trip to see my girl. And I would like to stay forever. It is so nice to sleep in a real bed and to wear washed clothes. But in a short while I think we shall..."

"... stop retreating, do you mean?" Her mother came into the kitchen and as always started to interrupt whoever was speaking.

"Sorry, no, Frau Schubert, we are retreating, that's the long and the short of it. You don't mind me saying so in this house?"

"Someone could hear you and then..." her mother said reproachfully.

"I trust everybody in this house," Heinrich answered and put an arm around Ruth again, "I trust Sturmbannführer Schubert and I trust his family. I can only stay four days. I'm keen to enjoy them. What comes next...at the front nobody knows."

"In the newspaper they say thousands of German

volunteers are digging trenches in East Prussia to stop the Russians." Her mother sounded defiant.

Heinrich hugged Ruth and smiled at her mother answering very slowly: "Yes, they are. But that won't do the trick. We are definitely in big trouble with this war. But don't talk to anybody about this. I would be in deep water and dead before the next bullet from a Russian could hit me."

She tried to get a grasp on what they were talking about in the kitchen that day. It was not yet clear to her what a war actually was and why her mother was in a mood to fight.

But the horses were grand. Their names were Eva and Egon. Eva was bay and Egon was white. Egon could be ridden; Eva was already used to pulling a cart. On the morning of his third day Heinrich promised to fetch Egon from the farm in the afternoon and let everybody have a ride in the grounds of Villa Caprice.

"I'm not worried. I am looking forward to the riding," she told Heinrich as she watched him cooking lunch with his famous Heinrich Müller sauce.

"Great!" Heinrich turned away from cutting onions, put his hands around her waist and lifted her up till she could look straight into his face. "Are you sure, little girl? Then I call you a brave girl."

He whirled her around twice, then put her down on the kitchen table. She saw her mother standing in the doorway. Heinrich got on cutting the onions.

"What are you doing here?" her mother hissed. "Heinrich you should not let the children disturb you!"

"We are having fun," Heinrich answered as he came back to her and stroked her hair. "Your little daughter is tough, isn't she? I like that. She will cut a good figure on a horse. Great child."

"I am not sure yet if I shall let the children ride. It's my turn first anyway. My husband always wanted me to become a rider. So today I'll give it a try. Will you be my teacher?"

"Of course, Frau Schubert!" Heinrich made a nice little bow. Then he winked at her.

A few hours later she was sitting on a horse for the first time in her life. Her mother had changed her mind and postponed the lesson. For safety reasons. Because a mother was needed for everything. Always. She wished Heinrich would stay forever.

———

A Courier 1944

In the mornings the house was empty again. Heinrich was back at the front, her sister back at school and her grandmother went for long walks because her nerves were not good. Her mother went out every morning to see if there was anything to buy for dinner in the grocery in Pörtschach or to visit the wife of Herr Meyer, the teacher. Herr Meyer was away fighting with her father. She would have liked to go with her mother and play with the two Meyer children who, like her, hadn't started school yet. But however often she asked to be taken her mother refused. She had to stay with her little brother, her mother said. Her mother did not like to take the two of them because she believed the little boy couldn't walk so far. But he could and it was only that her mother did not listen.

Ruth had to do a lot of cooking and washing and carrying water to the house. She knew very well that Ruth was missing Heinrich but was happy at the same time. She missed Heinrich too. He knew how to play in the forest or how to throw a ball over the hedge into the lake so that the ball landed with a great splash in the water and came floating back right to the place where they were standing. And that was even though they changed their standing places all the time. It was a secret how it happened. At any event Heinrich refused to give it away.

Frau Gruber was busy too but always took a break and offered her and her little brother a drink of water when they came to see her. She felt good sitting at Frau Gruber's table. There was only one room, the kitchen, and a tiny dark extension.

Frau Gruber's bed was behind a curtain and her clothes were hanging by the wall.

Frau Gruber waited for the postman every day. So did Ruth. Heinrich had promised all of them to write as soon as he got back to her father. But no letter arrived.

"We all make sacrifices for the final victory," her mother said, "I have not had a letter either. They are bombing our cities to block supplies to the front. But they cannot stop us. We are stronger than ever. That's what was emphasized on the radio."

Her mother always seemed to be a different person when she talked like this: "There will be a miracle. Germany believes this. Our letters will come through eventually. Hitler says we still have the strength and power to change our fate."

All her grandmother said after that speech was: "Will we never learn from our mistakes?"

She couldn't see what all this talking had to do with the letters that did not arrive.

One day a man in a uniform who was a courier brought a note, but it was not until the next day that she understood a note was like a letter. Her mother read the note, put it into her pocket and, after the courier had left, went on dusting the sitting room. The day passed as usual. At the dinner table that night her mother addressed Ruth all the time. Ruth had to answer questions about the household.

In the evening, since it was a Saturday, Ruth heated a lot of water and she and her sister and brother finally got a good wash. While she was putting on her night-dress her sister kept looking at Ruth. Her sister actually stared fixedly at Ruth.

"What's the matter?" Ruth asked.

Her sister went on looking straight into Ruth's face.

"You are staring at me," Ruth said, "why?"

Her sister now looked away and answered: "Ask mother."

The next morning Ruth was already in the kitchen, first as usual, when she went into the kitchen too. She could not sleep as long as the others.

"Come to me, I can do your hair before you sister comes," Ruth said. She had long hair which needed to be plaited into a pigtail. She could not do it by herself yet. Ruth did it very nicely.

When the pigtail was finished Ruth turned her round, looked into her eyes and said: "Now you look beautiful, my dear."

She saw tears in Ruth eyes and wondered why Ruth was crying when she spoke so kindly.

"Why are you crying?" she asked carefully. She was not sure about what she had seen. Ruth had been so happy all the time.

"Heinrich is dead. It was in the note that came with the courier. Your sister must have known before your mother told me. After you had gone to bed."

She wanted to give Ruth a kiss like she had seen a mother giving her child a kiss in her sister's schoolbook. But in their house nobody ever kissed anybody. Only Heinrich had kissed Ruth. But that was because he was in love.

She did not kiss Ruth. Ruth wiped her eyes and said: "It's alright. I'll be fine again in a while. But he was such a good man."

Yes, she thought, Heinrich had been a very good man. And very good company. Now he was dead and would never come back. Waiting for him was useless. Dead people never came back. She hoped she would learn later who had shot or bombed him. She felt very miserable.

She saw her mother for the first time that day when she herself was setting off to go to Frau Gruber to talk over what had happened. Her mother had had her breakfast in bed and was now dressed to go out. Her mother looked at her, expressionless, then as she reached the front door, shouted after her: "Don't go out without a cardigan!"

―――

Surrendering 1944

"It is a scandal," her mother said at the dinner table, just when she was looking forward to some discussion about how they would celebrate her siblings' birthdays which were coming up soon. "All these troops surrendering is a betrayal of the German people. That's all everyone was talking about in Pörtschach this morning."

"So we are finally coming to the end of the disaster." Her grandmother breathed deeply, as an expression of relief, she thought, and touched her little brother's hand.

"We are not!" Her mother spoke slowly, emphasizing every word, and looked very angry. "It is all because the English and the French make German prisoners talk on the radio. Those captured officers have been brainwashed. Why else would they advise their comrades to put down their weapons? It is a trick by the enemy. And incidentally it is forbidden to listen to foreign stations."

"I listen anyway," her grandmother said calmly.

"So!" her mother lengthened the one syllable. "That's interesting to hear."

Now her grandmother smiled a little, looked at her like she looked when she was going to tell an interesting story, and reported: "The English are dropping blue leaflets over the marching troops. From planes. It says on them the German soldiers should take off their helmets, keep hold of the leaflet and surrender. Then nothing will happen to them."

"I hope they stay devoted to the cause," her mother said.

"I'm sorry, but the fact is they do not." She noticed a tiny gleam in her grandmother's eyes.

Ruth was not following the conversation. Ruth was helping her little brother to cut a piece of the meat which her mother had brought home that day. Ruth said: "You're doing very well, my boy," although her little brother had not yet managed to cut anything by himself.

"Is father coming home soon or not?" Suddenly her sister was asking a question as though she had the right to steer the conversation. Her mother seemed disturbed by the enquiry and looked at the table cloth. Nobody spoke for a while.

"Well?" her sister asked just as vehemently.

Now her mother looked up and answered pleasantly: "I wish he was here just as much as you do, dear. But it will not happen soon. He is needed so badly out there. He is fighting hard. His only goal is to bring this war to a successful conclusion. You know he belongs to what is called a special task force. That's why he never takes days off. In a war you cannot take a holiday if you are seriously engaged in protecting mothers and children at home."

A few days later a second note came. Her father was wounded and coming home to make a full recovery.

At first she did not know how badly wounded her father was. Had he lost an arm or a leg, she wondered, like some men in Pörtschach who had come home from the war earlier and were walking on crutches now? She knew Heinrich was hit in the back and had died immediately. Ruth had been told that Heinrich had not suffered. But the men in Pörtschach had, she was sure.

At bedtime, her mother said that her father's car had

gone over a mine and exploded and his devoted comrades had saved him from burning to death.

———

Father **1944**

Her sister was allowed to accompany her mother to the military hospital. The two of them left after lunch and took the train to Klagenfurt. They always came home late. Ruth could not go along. Someone else was needed at home besides her grandmother. She discovered that Ruth would have liked to ask her father some questions about Heinrich, but her mother said all of that would have to wait till later.

Her mother brought greetings from her father but did not really explain how he was. Her sister said he had bandaged hands and bandages over his ears. He sometimes sat in the bed and he was able to speak. After a few days her sister let slip that her father wanted her mother to bring her and her little brother as well. She asked her mother if that was true.

"I put my foot down about that," her mother answered, looking very morose. "I mean I'm not taking you all the way to Klagenfurt. That would cause me a lot of trouble. But he wants you to come. And your brother later on as well." Her mother took a deep breath and went on: "In times of war men become very rude. He should realize that it is very hard for me to make the journey to Klagenfurt every day. And harder still taking children."

Two days later her sister was told to stay at home because her mother was taking only her to the military hospital. Her sister started to cry and carried on crying very hard for quite a while. When her mother finally told her sister to stop she actually did and said: "I couldn't keep it up any longer anyway."

The military hospital was closed when they arrived. Closed till four o'clock they were told.

"Why is it closed?" her mother asked the man at the desk in the hall, "I have come all the way from Pörtschach." Her mother was using her reproachful voice and she felt ashamed of it.

"The Gauleiter is here," the man said. "Nobody else can go in till four o'clock."

"But I know him," her mother insisted.

"Which of us doesn't?" the man answered and looked at her, smiling. "It is a question of security, madam."

Her mother took her hand and they went to a footpath around the park beside the hospital. "Oh, these Austrians," her mother said as they began walking under the big old trees. It was a long, boring walk around and around. Sometimes they sat on a bench, then walked again. First she had hoped her mother would talk about her father. How long he would stay with them and if he would stay in bed all the time. But all they talked about was the three ducks on the pond and she did not understand why her mother felt so sorry for these animals that had no shelter at night.

She knew her father would stay at least till after Christmas. "Then the war will be over," her grandmother had said. "The English had thousands of planes over Germany the other day. That means whole streets in the towns are gone. Have been wiped out I mean. Imagine for yourself, daughter, how many deaths that will have caused and how many more people are homeless now."

"Where did you hear that?" her mother asked.

"From the English."

"Are you still listening?"

Her grandmother smiled lightly.

At first her mother didn't seem to know what to say. Then she straightened herself up, and waving a finger at her grandmother and pausing after every word of the first sentence, said:

"Do not go near the radio when he is here! If anyone found out that the law was being flouted in this house it would mean death for him and for us too. Nobody is allowed to listen to all those lies the enemy puts about."

"Don't threaten me," her grandmother had said without dropping her smile. "You'd do better to prepare yourself for what's coming next. The victors won't treat SS people with kid gloves, I imagine."

She was surprised how vividly she always remembered this conversation. But then she always found it entertaining to hear her mother and grandmother quarrelling. Almost funny. But afterwards, when she recalled what had been said, it made her anxious. It was not so easy to work out who was right.

"Where will father sleep?" she asked her mother on their final round. She couldn't stand the silence anymore. If her mother did not want to talk about other things, she thought, then maybe talking about her father would be of more interest to her.

"With me, of course, in your bedroom," her mother answered. "You children will move downstairs. My room is far too small for a double bed."

This was bad news. She liked the children's room upstairs. It had several windows. The morning sun shone on her bed. In the evening she could see the red sky through the window beside her sister's bed. And later on all the stars. Her mother never closed the curtains because the three of them liked the stars so much. Sometimes she tried to tell her little brother a story about the stars, about a tiny one among all the big ones. But her sister said what she thought up was rubbish and threatened to shout for her mother if she didn't stop talking altogether. The room downstairs was dark and cold and never got any sun.

Her father was sitting in his bed and smiled at her very lovingly when they came into his room. His hands lay motionless on the duvet. She was allowed to give him a kiss and she tried to do it like she had seen Ruth giving Heinrich a kiss on the cheek. Her father told her she had grown a lot and was looking beautiful.

"Really?" she asked and tried to look nicer still. She had thought only her sister was beautiful. She liked her father very much although with his bandaged head he looked different from in the photo.

"We shall have a good time when I am home," her father said still looking at her, "are you able to ride a bike?"

Before she could start telling him about her ride into the lake her mother said: "I've been here for an hour. They wouldn't let me in because of the Gauleiter." Her mother still sounded annoyed. "I wonder who he was visiting."

Now her father broke into a deep laugh and his eyes shone with amusement. Then he looked at her mother for a while before he said: "Me, of course. The old sport. We had a nice chat. Gave me a real lift with his good news. The Japanese just destroyed the whole American fleet at Formosa. Remember the word 'Formosa', my girl." Her father turned towards her. "That word will come to stand for our final take-over."

On their way home her mother was quiet again. After a

while she plucked up the courage to ask: "When will our beds be brought down?" Every day she could still sleep upstairs was special now.

"Don't bother me with silly questions," her mother answered. "I really have more important things to sort out. Now that we have a future again."

———

A Family 1944

The days were different now her father was home. Particularly in the mornings she did not feel bored anymore. Nor lonely. To her astonishment she was not sent out of the room when her parents talked.

"Let her stay," her father said on the first day after his arrival when her mother was ordering them out: "Go! This is adult business. Children do not always have to know what grownups are talking about."

But her father contradicted his wife: "Children's minds improve whenever they think about things they don't understand. Hopefully, they will ask and…"

"Oh, stop," her mother cried, "I am tired of answering children's questions. You don't know how hard it is looking after them as a single mother. In a war! Without enough food! And everything else as well."

"I sent you as much as I could," her father replied, and she thought he looked confused about her mother's outburst. "It wasn't easy to get the ham. And the shoes for the girls. They cost me a whole day's absence from my lads. And, incidentally, we rarely get a proper meal or clean clothes out there. We don't sleep in featherbeds, you know, and people are dying all around us."

"We are under threat from planes," her mother replied." She had the impression her mother was immediately searching for arguments. "It is dangerous here as well. And I don't know how all this will end."

"It is heaven here, my dear." Her father actually laughed

when he spoke. "That's why I sent you to this place. Even I don't know exactly where the war will lead us. At the front we just try to survive each day as it comes, while you're teaching your children to swim. Think about that. And trust our Führer."

Sometimes when her father and her mother argued her mother started to cry, sometimes her mother reproached her father for not being so nice anymore. And for having wanted the war and...

"...and you agreed that Germany was a state without enough room and that something had to be done about it. We do have the extra territory now," her father said.

"We are losing it." Her mother spoke in her familiar wailing tone.

Now her father answered very seriously: "We'll get it back. Something is being prepared that I can't talk about. Trust me."

It was some time after this that the car stopped coming to take her father to the military hospital in Pörtschach to get his hands dressed. He was well able to walk that far, he said, and he would take her too if she wanted to walk with him. Her father had recovered the use of his hands by then but the awful new, red skin had to be looked after by a nurse. She was glad that there were bandages over his wounds. She did not like to touch his hands when they were uncovered. It did not bother her that he was not hearing very well. You only had to raise your voice.

"I'm taking the young lass with me to the hospital," her father shouted in the hall that morning. She was dressed and ready and Ruth was just handing her a woollen cap. It was a cold winter morning. Christmas was not far away.

Her mother came out of the dining room where she and

her grandmother had had a quarrel and asked in astonishment; "Why? She's fine here."

"Why not?" her father replied and winked at her.

"You are better on your own," her mother burst out.

"I don't think so." Her father waited for a reaction from her mother. As there was none he put on a funny voice: "The two of us will have a nice little excursion. And you and your son are going to build a snowman. That's what he just told me. Have fun too."

Her father took her hand and pulled her out of the house. Walking between the high walls of heaped-up snow on the drive beside him she heard her father saying: "I must confess the snowman was my idea. Your brother hadn't thought of it till then. Now she has to give him some attention. You see, my girl, I didn't lose my memory in the explosion. I still know how to make children happy." She silently agreed.

"By the way does your mother sometimes wear the Mothercross?" her father asked as they had reached the road and started to walk on the slippery snow towards Pörtschach.

"When she dresses to go out. But the band itches."

" So, so," her father murmured.

She wore woollen gloves and held her arm tight to her body. Her father reached out and took her hand.

"Warm my bandages," he said, "it is a cold winter. I wonder how my comrades are surviving out there. We have to do without so many things."

Her father sighed and did not look so happy anymore. Then he went on: "Your mother is spoiled. If she were still living in Germany now she wouldn't have time to behave like this."

The Nazi's Faith 1944

The last day her father had to go to the hospital was a sunny day. There were just three weeks to go till Christmas and it was not a cheering sight to see the snow melting rapidly. "Christmas without snow is nothing," her mother said as she fastened the yellow paper stars her sister had brought from school to the lamp over the dining table. Then, addressing her father: "If they decide today that you are well enough to go back to the front you won't go immediately, will you? I think I deserve a Christmas with a husband at home."

Her father smiled at her mother: "My dear, if they, as you call my superiors, say I have to go, no crying wife and children can stop me. I told you it's worse at the Plattensee. The Russians have been making progress while I have been twiddling my thumbs here. The boys need me over there."

Her mother's expression changed, she noticed. Now her face assumed a more understanding expression as she said: "Oh, I know very well how important officers are. But you should look after yourself too. Your ear drums are punctured. Your hearing has not got better. How will you avoid the bullets in time?"

"The boys will tell me. They saved my life. They'll go on looking after me, I assume."

She was in conflict with herself about the outcome of this morning at the military hospital. She wanted her father to be fine again. But she wanted him at home for Christmas as well.

"By the way," her father went on, "Christmas is not that important. Christmas is something for stupid people. See where the Jews have brought us with their religion. Hitler likes the solstice. That's what is catching on in Germany."

That could not be right, she thought. Her sister was talking all the time about Christmas celebrations at school and she herself had seen Santa personally in Berlin. Sent by Hitler.

"The Austrians think Christmas is very important," she heard herself saying then.

Her father touched her hair very gently: "The Austrians are Catholics, my girl. We let them have their faith. They are easier to handle that way."

She very wisely stopped herself asking what that was supposed to mean. Her mother would not allow her to have that sort of conversation with her father. "Are we leaving for the hospital now?" she asked instead.

Her father looked at his wrist and said: "Oh, we must be on our way if we are to make it in time."

"Let her stay," her mother insisted," you'll be faster without her and you'll get there in time. It is an important appointment today."

"She can take the bike."

Now it was her turn to say: "Oh." Riding her sister's bike was what she had dreamed of doing. Then she added: "But I am not allowed to."

"Your sister is at school, we can't ask her now. We shall tell her afterwards." Her father was heading towards the front door.

"She is very anxious about that bike," her mother said, "you should know your eldest daughter by now."

"We are in a hurry. We do need the bike. The roads are almost clear. Is there anything we should get from the shop other than what is on your list?"

Her father guided her out of the house. The last she saw was Ruth and her grandmother smiling. Her mother had already disappeared .

Finally a dream had come true. She was cycling on tarmac on her sister's beautiful bicycle. The year they moved into the Villa Caprice her father had said in a letter that his children should make a wish and he would send whatever they wished for from Italy. Her sister had cried: "A bicycle!" That's what she had wished for as well. It had been a long time since her fourth birthday and she had felt ready for cycling. At the Gauleiter's house some children had had beautiful bicycles. She couldn't stop watching them riding up and down the narrow road. And she had envied her mother when her mother's bike arrived with the furniture from Berlin.

"Then we shall wish for a tricycle for you," her mother had said, looking at her. "And a scooter for our boy here." Her mother smiled at her little brother. He showed no sign of pleasure. "Then we will own a nice little selection and you will have plenty of vehicles to entertain yourselves."

Two weeks later a soldier had arrived from Italy. He could not stay because he had immediately to go to Greece where her father now was. He brought a wooden scooter, a very small tricycle and a great bicycle that fitted her and her sister's age perfectly. The scooter would not roll on the gravel around the Villa. When she sat on the tricycle she could not get her knees under the handlebar and so she gave the thing to her brother who immediately stopped crying.

"All right, the two of you can share the bicycle," her mother said

"Oh no!" Her sister seemed ready to fight with everyone. "The bike is mine. Ask father!"

"Be nice to each other," her mother had said and gone into the house.

She had learned to ride on her mother's bike and liked to use it till the incident with the lake happened. She rode it into the lake. Then her mother did not let her have it anymore.

So, yes, she was in heaven riding beside her father to the military hospital that day. Her father walked very fast because he was in a hurry and she had to move her legs as fast as she could too because the cycle had no freewheel mechanism. But now and then the two of them exchanged happy glances.

———

Christmas 1944

Her father stayed for Christmas. She found out that he had only reluctantly accepted his doctor's decision to give his hands some more time to heal. When snow started to fall again her father went skiing with her mother although she heard him confessing to Ruth that his hands became painful from gripping the ski sticks. She felt sorry for him. But her mother had said he would be fine as long as they did not have to bring the children with them. Her father had got short skis for her sister, her little brother and herself. She was already practising on the drive. But her mother said taking the children would be no fun. They would get cold and tired and ruin her outing by crying and carping.

Her father skied with them on the drive. They didn't go that fast. They didn't actually get up much speed going down from the road to the house. But the three of them and the boys from the gate lodge had a good time. To her astonishment her father shook with fear when he stood on his skis, trembling and crying for help, and when he eventually went down the hill he often fell and they had to help him up and explain to him again and again that he had to keep his skis straight, not let his legs go out to the right and left until he was ready to fall onto his bottom to stop the ride.

Indoors it was quiet and boring. She did not see any preparations for Christmas. Her grandmother stayed in her room most of the time. Ruth talked about Heinrich with her father, and her mother said it was impossible to look forward to whatever celebration there might be because the war was not looking good.

She had just discovered that there were only eight more nights till Christmas Eve when an unforeseen joy broke out in the house. Her father came home from Pörtschach were he had met some comrades and collected her sister from school. His eyes were sparkling with delight. He took her mother in his arms and then Ruth and winked at her and her little brother, saying: "I have very good news. Oh, I am so happy. We finally got it going again. This morning our troops started an offensive on the western front to get back parts of Luxemburg. That will drive a wedge between the Allies. And when that is done the war will take a turn for the better."

"I don't think so!" Her grandmother's voice came from the kitchen door. "How can anybody still believe these lies? How can anybody still think Hitler is going to win this war? Why can't he give up now and make an end to all the suffering?"

She had never understood why her grandmother did not like Hitler. Her mother said everybody liked the Führer. He was making Germany a better country. But they all had to help him by not complaining about the current circumstances. Everything would be better after the war. They only had to believe it.

"Mother! Please! Don't talk about things you don't understand." To her surprise her mother didn't get angry. Her father looked at her grandmother in a friendly way as well and said: "You wait and see. Okay? We will show you what Hitler has in mind. With our fervent belief in victory we shall defeat everyone who tries to stop us making his plans come true."

"I'd better go back to my room and write that down," her grandmother said retreating to the staircase, "I have collected a lot of quotes like that already. I'll make a book of them when all this is over. The world will shake with laughter."

Although for a while there was talk about shooting and the new weapons the Germans would have against the enemy, the joy stayed in the Villa Caprice. Her father closed the door to the sitting room and put up a sign that said: 'No entry.' Then he started making a lot of noise inside, sometimes she heard hammering and some other noises nobody could identify. Ruth said he was making the presents for Christmas and that they would all have a good time on Christmas Eve. There would even be a tree this time now that their father was with them.

On the last night before Christmas Eve her father put them to bed as he often did. She begged him to play 'confusion' first because it was so funny. First he did not know what she was talking about, then he understood but said: "No. I am not in the right mood for it."

"But we are!" her sister and her little brother cried. So her father put her little brother onto his shoulder and said: " Right! To bed you go." But her father did not head for the dark room where they slept now. He went in the direction of the kitchen.

"No, no." Her little brother cried splitting his sides laughing, "that's not our bedroom!"

"Then it's here." Her father touched the dining room door.

"No, no!" cried her little brother, "That isn't it either! Walk on!"

Her mother stopped the game. "Dear," she shouted, "don't mess about. The children are far too old for such silliness. Put them to bed. I want you to sit down with me. I am actually very worried."

"I love father," her little brother said later before he fell asleep, " he promised to build a sailing boat with me. After the war. It will have a motor too so we can go sailing when there is no wind."

"Baby talk." Her sister spoke in a knowing voice. "Forget it. Everything has changed today, mother told me. Father will not be taking us to England and nor will he be rebuilding the house in Berlin. The battle on the Western front has been lost. Now you know."

"Then we'll stay here at the lake," she said. She really did want to stay forever. But her sister answered: "Ha, you don't get it. We shall be in the hands of the enemy soon with no free will. Because we are SS. And they hate the SS."

She felt miserable over Christmas. Although her father had built her a wooden dolls' pushchair, which was a surprise because she did not play with dolls, and although they really did have a Christmas tree, even if there were only five candles on it, still she could not feel any joy. Her father talked about the Plattensee where he would go in a while and how hard the fighting would be there.

"Don't expect letters when I am gone," he warned her mother, "I shall be happy if I get some sleep now and then."

"Stay, please!" Her mother begged. "Find an excuse. The war will be over shortly."

"Don't talk like that," her father answered, and she realised her father was really angry. "That's not what we need to keep going. Have faith! We are NOT finished yet. That's why I am needed out there."

Her father left on the second day of the new year. Her mother cried but stayed in the house and did not allow the three of them to go with him to the road where a jeep was waiting to take him away. She heard the jeep speeding away in the direction of Klagenfurt.

Ruth was busy in the kitchen after that but did not want to talk. It seemed to her Ruth was thinking of Heinrich and the time he had gone away and that was why she didn't want her around. Her grandmother had left the house early that morning, her little brother was in his bed again because it was cold in the house, except in the dining room where the cast iron stove was lit . But her sister was in there already, curled up with her mother in an armchair, and shouted at her: "Go away. We are having a serious talk just now!"

Her mother smiled at her but did not say a word. So she closed the door again. Then she remembered that Frau Gruber had got some wool and had promised to teach her how to knit. She left the house without a coat and was happy to find Frau Gruber at home.

———

Herr and Frau Von Mattes 1945

There was no letter from her father in the weeks after he left, just as he had warned them. Nor one for her birthday. She thought it was an important day. She was six years old now and old enough to go to school. But it was still winter. There would be spring first and then summer and then she would start school. This had been her greatest wish for a long time now. To be with other children and getting attention from the teachers seemed to her the best thing anyone could hope for. She couldn't actually believe that teachers answered all the questions children at school asked. In her mind she already had a long list of complicated problems which she was really keen to sort out.

"When I'm at school can I ask why adults always focus on one thing and want to talk about that all the time?" she asked her sister one evening when they were undressing for bed.

Her sister pulled a disgusted face and said: "Stupid questions are not accepted, of course."

Her birthday came... and her mother was very depressed and turned it into an awful day because on the radio they said more towns in Germany had been bombed out or partly destroyed, that refugees were coming in long treks from the east through frost and ice and snow, that the enemy was becoming bolder and bolder and that they should all protect themselves by digging trenches to stop the enemy troops which were all determined to wipe out Germany. Now she was six she walked around with her head high so as to look more grown up. And then one day, by a happy chance, she learned of something before her sister did.

The thing was: Herr and Frau Mattes, the owners of the house, wanted to move in.

"That is impossible," her mother said to Ruth and her grandmother in the kitchen. "The Gauleiter confiscated the Villa for us. We have a right to live here on our own."

"But Mattes' house was bombed last year and they are still living in the cellar there," her grandmother said, clearly not put off by her mother's laments. "It's understandable that they should want to move into their second house."

Ruth looked up and remarked: "Actually they live with friends now. Six people in two rooms. The cellar was too wet. We have to let them come."

She was astonished about Ruth. Ruth mostly agreed with her mother.

"We are in a war," her mother answered vehemently, "we all have to lower our sights."

She saw her grandmother smile slightly as she gave her opinion: "Upstairs they would have their own toilet. A kitchen can easily be set up in the small bedroom you were in. I'll help them carry water up the stairs. Now you can see how clever it was to build the staircase for this house on the outside."

"You are sixty five years old," her mother said, "you should not...."

"But so are they! We shall just have to make do for the next few weeks anyway. The reality is that the war..."

"Oh, stop it." Her mother seemed really furious now. "I am sick of your prophecies. This is a problem for men. I am going to write a letter to him. He may decide what to do. He can phone the Gauleiter and get advice."

Her grandmother made to leave the kitchen but stopped

at the door and seemed almost unable to restrain her anger: "You know yourself where he is now all hell has been let loose. I actually thought the courageous wives of the Waffen SS soldiers would be guarding the backs of their courageous troops."

It was only a short while later that Herr and Frau Mattes moved in. Her mother had got a second begging letter from Klagenfurt and finally agreed to let the two elderly people move in. "But the terrace and the island are ours," her mother said, "and we keep the garden and the boat. They may use the bridge if they still go swimming."

"It is their house," her grandmother had muttered. But only she heard it.

Her mother came to sleep with them in the dark bedroom. Her grandmother kept her room upstairs and she liked to spend time with her grandmother there and admire the view. Her grandmother enjoyed seeing the Karawanken mountains as well and said that it was her only pleasure in the Villa Caprice. Ruth still slept in her little attic refuge and looked happy about that.

Her grandmother welcomed the Mattes with a bunch of kindling sticks gathered specially for them in the woods nearby and helped to start the first fire upstairs. The stairs to the first floor ran outside along the wall beside the main entrance of the Villa. She heard her mother saying that this made it possible to keep the two families entirely separate and that they should keep it that way.

"So you, the three of you," her mother said after the lorry which had brought the Mattes' possessions had left, "you stay downstairs now, all the time. We are not going to socialize with them."

Every morning after that she went up the stairs and

stood on the landing for a while to look at the lake and the mountains. The entrance door to the upper rooms was always closed. Nobody noticed her there as she listened to the voices of the Gauleiter's children. Their laughter and shouting came to her from the spit of land that reached into the lake in front of the Villa Caprice. The Gauleiter's family was living there. Once, when she had been in a peculiar, lonely mood, she had shouted to these children and she was sure they had answered back. But her mother said it was only an echo.

Herr and Frau Mattes were nice people. They smiled at her when they happened to meet outside. They stayed upstairs most of the time. She never heard them talking. Sometimes they left early in the morning and soon came back quietly with some shopping bags. They never strolled through the garden to the lake or looked after their boat which was now hanging in the boathouse a meter or so above the water. It was a wide old-fashioned boat with a beautiful curved iron railing around the double backseat. In the summer that seat had been hers and her little brother's when Ruth and her mother rowed out with them and they jumped into the lake for a swim. Her sister did not like swimming and stayed in the boat. Her little brother also remained behind because he could only swim under water beside the bridge. She herself was already a good swimmer but her mother insisted on her wearing the swimming belt made of cork.

One day Frau Mattes gave her an apple when she met her at the pump. She knew how heavy a bucket full of water was and had politely offered to carry one of the two Frau Mattes had just filled.

"My mother always lets me help Ruth," she said when Frau Mattes shook her head.

"Your mother should not do that," Frau Mattes answered, "Water is too heavy for a girl your age. Come, have this."

Frau Mattes took a scarlet apple out of her apron pocket and said: "Eat it now. Do eat it here. I want to be sure."

They could not go on talking. There was the sound of an engine in the air. They both looked up. Frau Mattes frowned and ordered: "Run, girl! Into the house with you!"

She knew that noise in the sky very well. A low flying aeroplane was coming nearer. That happened often now. "They are coming from Italy," her mother had said, "instead of bombing innocent people here they now attack us personally."

As they approached the house the pilots would fly lower and lower and then shoot into the windows. The safest place then was on the staircase into the cellar and down in the cellar which was under the dark bedroom.

"You have to run too," she said to Frau Mattes with a mouth full of sweet apple, "why do you never come to the cellar?"

"I have been told it is yours," Frau Mattes answered with a peculiar smile. "But we are fine in the hallway upstairs beside the chimney. We see friends in these chaps anyway. But you cannot understand that yet."

While she waited in the cellar for the attack to end, she wondered if she would be able to understand what Frau Mattes was saying if she were at school already. Her grandmother could probably explain it to her. But her grandmother had gone out early this morning after a row with her mother about things to do with the war. Her grandmother had almost cried when Ruth told them what people were saying in Pörtschach. So many people were on the run from the east of Germany and so many of them were dying of hunger and the severe cold. Her grandmother wanted Hitler to finish the war but her mother said everything would come to a good end. Hitler had now called up all the old men to the front as well. That was when her grandmother had reached for her hat and coat and left the house.

As she sat in the cellar she hoped her grandmother would find shelter somewhere else and come back safely. She hoped the pilots would not spot her and shoot her.

———

The Casualties Train 1945

The school in Pörtschach closed. It was made into a military hospital. Her sister was at home all day and had nothing else to do but watch her and her little brother and report to her mother whenever they did something wrong. But one morning was different. Her sister was gone to see a friend when her mother heard that a train full of casualties had stopped outside Pörtschach. Just across the field on the other side of the road.

"The school is overcrowded," she heard her mother saying to Ruth," they just don't know where to put all these wounded soldiers. I am going to bring coffee and sandwiches to them."

She ran to the road. Frau Mattes and her grandmother were already standing there. In the distance she saw a train standing just at the end of the field across the road. It was a long train and she saw the red crosses on the side of the wagons. She knew there were also red crosses on the top.

"Those crosses don't protect the wounded," Frau Mattes said to her grandmother. The two women were on good terms, she had noticed, but was sure her mother did not know.

"You mean they are in danger of being attacked by planes as well?" her grandmother asked.

"They are. It has happened too often that the Germans have been carrying troops and weapons under the protection of the red cross symbol. That's why the English and Americans don't trust the German Red Cross any more. It's another case of Mister Hitler breaking the mould of what it is to be human." Frau Mattes sighed and then smiled at her grandmother. "You are not offended, are you?"

Her grandmother smiled back and said: "For many years now I have been ashamed to be German."

She found the conversation difficult to comprehend and went back to the kitchen where her mother greeted her with the words: "You have to help me. I have used up almost all the coffee your father sent because he knows I cannot live without it. But today I have to do without. We are all in distress and the most vulnerable must come first."

Her mother took the basket with the sandwiches Ruth had just made, packed all their cups in it and handed her the big milk can. "Take that, pull yourself together and come on before the coffee gets cold."

They went up the drive, her grandmother and Frau Mattes were gone, crossed the road and stepped into the field. She was cold because she had no coat on. Her shoes soon got wet, then her socks and she felt altogether miserable. The milk can was awfully heavy and she had the feeling she would not make it to the train.

"Come on," her mother said impatiently, "that train has been standing there all night already. There is no hope of getting these casualties into proper beds soon. The school is full. I could cry. Lift your feet. The grass is wet."

There was a noise in the sky. A familiar sound coming from behind her. And then the 'tak, tak, tak' of shooting.

"The low flying planes!" her mother shouted, "we have to get to shelter."

She saw her mother throwing herself on to the ground and then rolling under a big bush in the hedge around the field.

She looked around her. Where to put the milk can? The

ground was not smooth, there was tall, stiff grass growing here and there. The can could tip over. The coffee would be gone. The 'tak, tak, tak' was nearer now.

"Come here," she heard her mother shouting, "here I am. Put the can down and come."

Her mother's voice sounded angry now. She stamped the milk can into the ground, ran towards the bushes and bent down. There was hardly any space beside her mother. She broke a branch, hurt one of her fingers and eventually lay down near her mother like under a roof. The 'tak, tak, tak' was still coming nearer. Then it was directly over them. She could see between two branches that soil was being catapulted into the air. She felt her mother very close behind her. They did not move. But with contempt in her voice her mother said: "They shoot at casualties. They shoot at women and children. That's the way they try to win the war."

She did not listen. There was no room in her head to take in words. The shooting went on. She watched the milk can. It was still standing beside a tall clump of grass that ought to keep it upright. So the coffee was still safe. The thought gave her some relief. Then the noise of the planes and the shooting decreased and slowly disappeared. Her mother took a deep breath as she pushed against her back and said: "They're gone. Get the can."

But she did not move. She heard a plane coming back. Then she saw it. It flew a circle in the sky just above the train, came steeply down and the machine gun spat. There were noises of breaking glass, things crashing and falling, there was screaming. But very suddenly it was all over. The plane was gone, the voices became silent.

"Now! Go!" her mother commanded, "get the coffee!" And added: "I feel totally exhausted."

They walked towards the middle of the train. At the far end of the line of carriages she could see a crowd of soldiers helping each other to leave the train.

"They've been hit," her mother said calmly and walked on straight till they reached the train. A minute later her mother's voice sounded almost happy as she exclaimed: "Here we are. Look how their faces light up when they see us."

Just in front of them a train window had opened and a soldier with a bandage around his head and over one eye stretched out his arms and shouted: "Here are some angels coming. Come straight ahead and stop right under our window, ladies! Whatever you're bringing, it's for us here in this bloody cage. Am I right?"

"You are, Norbert, you are" came an answer from several voices inside. But she could not see into the carriage. The window was too high above her.

Hearing these clear German voices her mother looked more delighted and shouted back: "It is for you and your comrades. We can't do more to thank you for what you have done for us."

She thought then how good her mother was at acting. The Samaritan approaching the helpless victim. Her grandmother had read them a story about a good person like that. Now her mother was playing that part and soon everything they had brought had vanished through the window. The windows on the right and the left opened too but were shut again after her mother shook her head vigorously.

She looked to the end of the train. Some soldiers were lying in the grass, some were walking around and there was a lot of shouting. The soldier who did the talking and had taken the sandwiches and the cups of coffee for his comrades in the compartment followed her eyes and then remarked to her mother: "We were lucky here. The Tommies couldn't do a lot of damage with their manky planes."

While her mother was asking questions about the front she jumped up and down to keep herself warm. Her feet were ice cold and she wanted to go home. But her mother went on chatting and then, yes, bantering with the soldier. She wondered how many injured were lying in that compartment. The sandwiches were gone so quickly and the coffee too. Finally her mother said they had to leave. The soldier started a thank you speech on behalf of all of them.

"Can I give the little girl a kiss?" Suddenly there was a second face at the window. She thought how friendly the tall man's eyes were as he looked at her. A jacket was hanging over his right shoulder and blood was all over his shirt on his chest.

"Of course you may." Her mother bent down, wrapped both arms around her legs and there she was swinging through the air to be presented to the man. They looked at each other. She liked him. As though talking to himself he said: "I have a daughter your age. I shouldn't have taken your food. But I want to see my daughter again."

He kissed her on the cheek and because her mother was still holding her up she could look through the window into the carriage. The narrow space was fitted with several beds on top of each other on both sides. She saw bearded men with blood stained bandages lying there. Some looked at her, some seemed to be asleep, one was lying naked on his side, his face to the wall. One of his legs was missing, the dressing on the stump was red all over. The soldier who had kissed her looked backwards at his comrade, than back at her and with his quiet, small voice said: "He will be fine." Then, addressing her mother, he added: "He went mad. He wouldn't let us cover him even if we had something clean."

On their way home her mother was in good spirits and talked about how well they had been received.

In the evening her mother smiled at Ruth and her sister: "I got real satisfaction out of my mission today. It was a great feeling being so helpful. But..." her mother's expression now changed to a heavy, inward sadness... "it is hard to see all these poor soldiers, these poor casualties."

"You started it! All of you in your blindness," her grandmother remarked without emphasis, not looking up from her knitting.

———

The Lord Mayor 1945

She was looking forward to Easter. Her grandmother had promised her sister, her little brother and herself that she would bring them to the small forest on the far side of Pörtschach. Ruth was to come as well because there would be a lot of Easter eggs to carry home. But that would only be after they had searched hard and long for the eggs, her grandmother had said. If anyone wasn't willing to make a big effort then they should stay at home.

She busied herself thinking about how great the day would be and how triumphantly she would place egg after egg in the basket they took with them. It had already been padded for the purpose with green thick wool.

But then, one morning in the middle of the week before Easter, a man walked down the drive and went up to the front door of the Villa Caprice. She was sitting under the Big Tree watching a flock of birds that flew round and round over the boathouse. She heard her mother shouting: "Hallo! What a great surprise. Oh, do come in please." Her mother's voice always went higher and higher when she was delighted about something. So her mother knew this man. Her mother must have met him in Pörtschach where she was never taken.

The man wiped his feet on the outside doormat and slowly went in. The door stayed open. Her mother had already disappeared into the house. She looked back at the birds and wondered for a while if she should go in and see who this man was. She decided against it. There were no children in the house. Her sister had gone to see a friend as she so often did, her brother was with the neighbours who were running a small hotel and often gave him something to eat. Anyway her mother would send her out again immediately. Her mother would rather keep this man to herself. Her mother wouldn't even let Ruth or her grandmother sit with this man. As she thought this, she realised how completely familiar she was with her mother's attitudes, how deeply these attitudes influenced her own behaviour. For her all that mattered was not to upset her mother. An upset mother was someone you could not reach. A feeling of loneliness would follow. Even her little brother had mentioned something like that one evening in their bedroom, but her sister had stopped their talk by threatening them with: "Be quiet now or I'll call mother. And then you will see."

The birds made a last round over the boathouse and disappeared in the direction of Klagenfurt.

"That's the Mayor of Pörtschach, the man who just went into your house." Fritzi, the younger boy from the gate lodge, suddenly said beside her, " you are honoured. He wouldn't come to see my mother. Don't you feel proud now?"

Now she remembered that that man, the Mayor, had brought them to the Gauleiter's home. He had welcomed them at the station when they arrived from Posen.

She looked at Fritzi. She did not know what to answer. But she knew he was admiring her. That was a strange feeling. Fritzi was so much older than she was. She got up.

"There's your sister coming. Just in time," Fritzi went on, "I better go. She doesn't like me."

Her sister brought her little brother, who was carrying a paper bag with a half loaf of bread .

Her sister looked at the house and asked: "Why are you

standing around? Isn't lunch ready?" And in a bossy tone added: "I want my lunch now."

"The Mayor is visiting mother. We'd better wait." Of course her sister would laugh at her words.

And sure enough: "Rubbish," her sister shouted, "I shall go in. He was so nice when he came to welcome us at the station that time. Come on!" Her sister gave the order to her little brother and took a few steps towards the house, then stopped. The Mayor and her mother had appeared in the doorway. She saw the two shaking hands and she heard the Mayor saying: "Always at your service! Of course, Madam."

The Mayor went up the drive as though he was in a hurry, not looking at them. When he reached the road he went even faster. By then she had recognised his face. This man had not smiled when he had greeted her family at the station. Although his words had sounded friendly he had shown no emotion in his face. She remembered very well how unwelcome she had felt at the time.

"He's gone," her sister remarked, "hard luck. I would have liked to shake hands with the Mayor. That's something you could tell them about at school."

She followed her sister and little brother to the house. As they reached the bottom of the steps they saw that their mother was still standing in the doorway. They went up the few steps. Their mother was quietly waiting for them. Before she could make up her mind what kind of mood she was seeing on her mother's face, her mother addressed the three of them: "Come in and listen: You have to behave very well now. Because I am very sad. Your father is dead."

The Tito 1945

After her father's death her mother behaved differently. Her mother was worrying and complaining all the time. That made her worry too. But she did not dare to talk about her anxieties. Her mother had said life for children at her age was fine. They escaped all the hard blows adults had to bear and could be happy everywhere and all the time.

Now her mother did not talk of the Wunderwaffe anymore. The miracle weapon vanished. "We are losing the war," her mother said.

"Then I can go home," her grandmother answered. "They will not keep us here in Austria anyway. The occupiers."

Her mother looked alarmed. "The Austrians joined the Third Reich," she explained with a hard voice, "they are in it."

"But you are in command," her grandmother said, "Did anyone give this house to you voluntarily? No. You took it."

"Frau von Mattes had a second house in Klagenfurt."

"Yes, she did have. But that is bombed now. Gone. And because of that sad event you and your late war-hero kindly let her move into the attic of her own house here. It came as an order from the Eastern front. Oh, the Germans are so perfect."

"Frau von Mattes is fine up there," her mother said. "She may come down whenever she wants to. We are all in the same boat."

"She would hammer a hole into your boat if she could be sure to survive."

Some days later at lunch her mother, her grandmother

and Ruth, the adults in other words, were having a discussion about the forthcoming take-over by the enemy.

"We do not have to be worried. The English are already nearby," her grandmother said, "they will occupy this part of Austria. The will not do us any harm."

"But the Tito will," her mother said with an angry expression on her face. Her mother was always annoyed with her grandmother. "If the Tito comes we all will be massacred. We'd better drown ourselves before they arrive."

"Why?" her sister asked calmly. "Why will they do that?" Her sister was allowed to join in debates at the table. She and her brother had to be quiet. Because they were too small to know anything. Her sister was only two years older than she was. So eight years of age meant being almost an adult, being six did not count at all.

"Yes, why?" Ruth looked puzzled . "How will the Tito know that we are Germans?"

"And the family of a Waffen SS Sturmbannführer as well?" her grandmother remarked.

"We have sunk all fathers things in the lake," her sister said," there are only the books in the boathouse left." Her sister sounded proud to throw in such an intelligent argument.

Her mother shook her head. "The Austrians will tell them."

"No wonder," her grandmother said.

"Would you please shut up?" Her mother put her cutlery down and looked at her grandmother boiling with rage. "You would be dead already had I not asked you to come and live with us here. Starved to death. Up there in North Germany they eat sugar beet, day and night. Nothing else. For months. Your brother doesn't write anymore."

"I know". Her grandmother sounded very calm. " At least I would not have died as a Nationalsozialist."

When they had got up from the table she asked her mother: "Can I swim?"

"With your belt, yes." her mother answered. She hoped her mother would say something more. But her mother followed her sister and started talking about her sister's homework.

All afternoon she was thinking about what she had heard at the dining table. She walked around in the garden. She went to the boathouse and looked at the lake. The water seemed cold. The waves were higher than on normal windy days. Although it was spring swimming would not be easy. Even with her swimming belt she thought she might not be able to reach the peninsula opposite where the Gauleiter was living with his family.

In the evening her mother was in no better mood . But the adults did not talk about the Tito again. Her mother sent her sister , her brother and herself to bed early. When they had undressed and were lying in their beds their mother came to the door and said: "Good night. I don't want to hear any noise. Behave. Go to sleep now. Life is already hard enough for me. I cannot bear naughty children on top of it all."

She heard her sister and her brother talking for a while. Her brother was asking little boys questions. Her sister was giving answers like a grown up person.

"I am hungry," her brother said, "was it in the newspaper that we can only have one potato each?"

"Mother says we only have a few potatoes left," her sister answered," they may not give us any after the war."

"Is Adolf Hitler a king?" Her brother seemed to long for a story.

"Hitler is our Führer. The leader."

"So he doesn't have a crown?"

Her sister gave a short laugh. Then there was silence. Her brother apparently was reconsidering whether he should still share the common admiration of the Führer or let him go. As she was thinking this he suddenly asked: "What is massacring?"

"Making dead," she heard her sister explain with a high clear voice, "butchering, slaughtering."

At this moment in the darkness of the sleeping room she was sure that her brother would start crying. He did not. She could hear him breathing. Her sister seemed to notice his struggling for air as well. "Sleep now," her sister commanded. "You heard mother."

She felt released when it was finally quiet in their room. There was an urgent need to think something over. All the possibilities of the argument at lunchtime had to be considered, many questions answered. Would to be massacred be more frightening than to drown? She was sure her mother thought so. Adults new everything better. But how could one drown when one was well able to swim? Did you have to have stones fastened to your body? It was strange to recall what had happened several days before. Her mother and Ruth had put stones into the pockets of her father's heavy black coat. The coat she liked so much. The one with the cape over the shoulders. She could easily remember her mother's voice when they came back in the boat reporting that the coat sank immediately to the bottom of the lake. So did her father's pistols and the other things. But the books floated. They had to be fished out of the water again. She had seen the books this afternoon in the boathouse. Ruth and her mother had put them on the benches there along the walls. It was then that her mother had said: "Sinking them has failed. The books will have to dry fully, then we can burn them. They all contain SS details. Too dangerous to keep. They would give away who your father was."

Her sister and her brother were asleep. She thought she could go on more calmly now sorting out her actual problem. The drowning.

'I cannot drown,' she told herself, 'I shall float like the books did. My belt will keep me on the surface of the water.' Then real fear crept into her body. Her mother might not allow her to bring the belt. She would sink immediately. They would not even have to fasten a stone to her body. This thought took her breath away. She gasped. She folded her hands and pressed them hard. Then it occurred to her she would have to bring the belt secretly. Yes! But where to hide it? Everyone had always seen it when she was wearing the belt over her swimsuit. No, her plan was not yet ready.

She thought hard for some time but was eventually able to relax. There was nothing to be afraid of anymore. Of course this time they all would sit in the boat in their ordinary clothes. Her mother and the others would not detect that she was wearing her swimming belt under her dress. She would take advantage of her habit of always being the last to jump into the water when they went swimming. She would jump, pretend to drown - and swim away.

Now she was not lost in her brooding anymore. She felt better. She pulled the eiderdown over her head and imagined herself swimming through the reeds to the neighbour's shore, reaching their bridge, climbing out of the water and knocking at their back door. She would be safe then. They would look after her. Thinking these thoughts she started to weep, carefully, so as not to make a noise that could be heard by her sister. She wept. She went on weeping. She felt so sorry for the little orphan.

———

The Liberators 1945

In the morning a few days later there was an unusual noise coming from the road.

"The English have arrived!" Fritzi reported the news from outside through the kitchen window. "The war is over. Are you leaving now?"

Her sister was sitting at the kitchen table reading a school book and having her hair plaited, but she now ran out of the kitchen. She herself was stopped by Ruth.

"Let me do your hair as well." It struck her how different her nanny's voice sounded. Indeed, Ruth was smiling in a surprising way as she went on: "You won't miss anything. By the sound of it, there is a whole army coming." Ruth took a deep breath and added: "That's it then. Thank God."

Wrapped up in the excitement of the morning she merely registered that her mother was cleaning the dining room and was putting the chairs on top of the table. She could not see her mother's face and didn't want to see it either. All she wanted was to see the tanks and these soldiers, that her mother called enemies. She wanted to form her own opinion. She was six years old now. Her grandmother had her own opinion too.

As she ran up the drive she heard Fritzi, Ernsti and her sister calling towards the jeeps and tanks: "Please, please, chocolate." They shouted English words. She knew it was English. Frau Gruber knew the language and sometimes listened to the English radio station. But it was a secret and she mustn't mention it at home.

A tank stopped, a hatch on the top opened and first a soldier's head appeared, then shoulders and arms poked out of the heavy, dirty vehicle. The soldier raised his arms and then it happened: a big shower of small packets in pretty coloured wrappers flew from his hands. A second later the end of the drive was covered with sweets and bars of chocolate. She had never seen such treasure. Her sister and the boys started to gather up the treats. Her little brother came running to help. She felt glued to the spot but managed to meet the soldier's eye. He smiled. There was no doubt about it: the enemy soldier had smiled at her! He was friendly! She could see that. The way he held up his hands to let her know he had no more treats to throw told her he meant well towards her. As she was realising this it struck her again how incapable she was of understanding a war.

At lunch time Tito's men arrived too. As they passed their house they fired into the air.

The vehicles looked old and unfit for going very far. From the kitchen window they noticed that the Titos did not wear real uniforms. "They are partisans" her mother said, "they are taking advantage of our war. Let's wait calmly to see what the English will do."

Like the English troops, Tito's men headed for Pörtschach. She stayed in the kitchen after her family had left it. She sat at the table. She did not know what to think. What to do. Outside the roaring of the Tito vehicles could still be heard. There was the danger. Her mother had shrugged. Her mother seemed not to be afraid anymore. But how could her mother know? The thought occurred to her that her mother was only pretending to be calm. In order to prepare the drowning in secret.

Tito's men passed the Villa Caprice again a few hours

later, this time in the opposite direction. Again she saw their waving flags but could make nothing of what was written on their vehicles in big letters.

"I tell you. I am able to read," her sister said proudly, "they're announcing they will be back soon."

"They will not!" Her mother protested, turning round from the cooker. "The English occupied Pörtschach first. I am sure we will get along well with the English. I am an officer's widow, after all. They will protect us."

"You shouldn't be too sure," she heard her grandmother saying from the kitchen door. "After all the scandalous things they have had to endure from you." Her grandmother stepped into the hall but came back and added with unusual anger in her voice: "It is too early for forgiveness."

The rest of the day she wondered why her mother was so sure the English would be friendly. Her family was still suspect, with dangerous books lying to dry in the boathouse.

That evening they started eating the English soldiers' gifts of sweets. For the first time in her life she ate chocolate, although her mother insisted she had once before had some pieces out of Hitler's Santa's Christmas sack. But she could only remember sweets and biscuits.

So far the Titos had not come back. "The danger is over," her mother said, as she and her little brother were sitting on the floor beside her grandmother's armchair. Her mother sat at the dining table and was going through some papers and photos, tearing some of them up. Her little brother watched with interest. Her sister came in with a book and occupied the second armchair.

"Ruth will want to sit there," her little brother said.

"Ruth has gone to Pörtschach," her sister answered and curled up in the comfortable seat, "she can't wait to see what is going on there. She and Anni will be delighted to meet some soldiers."

Her mother's face lit up. "Naturally they will. But I am going to let the English settle first. In a couple of days I shall try to meet some of them. I am sure there must be an officer who will understand our situation and help us to go home."

Her grandmother put down her needlework and placed her hands on her little brother's head and her head, addressing her mother in a measured tone: "The war is not yet over, my dear daughter. Hitler is not yet captured. But I am sure he is anticipating his last minutes with great dignity."

While she was puzzling out what the last word could mean her mother seemed not sure what to answer. Her grandmother went on, now looking at the ceiling:

"You know yourself that Germany is bombed to blazes. There is no transport, no food, no roof over the heads of so many people. How will your new English friend be able to help you go home to Berlin?"

"Berlin?" her mother asked. She saw real disorientation in her mother's face. After a while her mother went on: "The Leibstandarte housing complex is gone. Didn't you know? We all have to go to your place in Kiel. Thank God the house was spared while the ones on both sides of it burnt down."

It began to occur to her that there were a few things she didn't know about either. Nobody had told her the house where she was born was not there anymore and that they were going to Kiel, not to England, and obviously not back to Berlin.

Her grandmother's face went white and the hand on

her head trembled. The room was silent for a while. Her sister looked up from her book in astonishment.

"There isn't enough room for all of us." Her grandmother spoke again. Now stressing her words a little: "It is a three room apartment as you will remember. There is no bathroom, only a tap in the kitchen and the toilet is on the landing in the stairwell. And as you also know very well my brother and his daughter and her family are already living there. I have just heard that Dolly has been able to borrow a grand piano to go on giving lessons so she can support all of them. Do you know how much space a grand piano takes up in a room of 18 square metres?"

"We have no choice." Her mother shrugged. "In these hard times people have to share. And would you please give some consideration to how much I have already lost because of the war? I need some comfort."

Now she noticed her little brother was going to cry. She got up and took him into the kitchen and played cards with him till it was time to go to bed. When her little brother saw that her grandmother was on her way to her room upstairs he begged for a story. For the first time her grandmother said: "Sorry, no! I am very tired."

Her mother looked astonished and seemed ready to interfere. But her grandmother was quicker and, pointing her finger resolutely at her mother, said: "You do it! You are one of those mothers of the Reich who have been so mightily praised. You tell them a story. A happy one, of course. Or is there something more urgent than that?"

She was sure there were tears in her grandmother's eyes as she opened the front door and hastened towards the stairs.

The Boat House 1945

"They won't take our house," her mother said one day at breakfast after the English had settled in Pörtschach and started confiscating the houses along the shore of the Wörthersee for their officers. She knew that a man in an office in Pörtschach had told her mother that her family was under no circumstances allowed to leave Austria without permission. She was glad to know they would stay in the Villa Caprice for the time being.

"If you are talking of this house" her grandmother remarked, pointing to the ceiling of the dining room, "then I have to remind you that it belongs to the lady and the gentleman upstairs."

"Oh, do shut up." Her mother's forehead wrinkled. "I am the one who takes it to heart. And I am telling you that no English officer will want to live in this house."

"But it is a beautiful house," her sister claimed.

"Yes it is, indeed!" Her little brother nodded energetically.

Ruth did not say anything and went on buttering a slice of bread and put honey on it. Her mother had brought the honey from the farmer Franz. Her mother used to visit him now and then and was always excited when she came back. Farmer Franz lived on his own in a big house high up in the mountains and had several men working for him.

"If someone comes to see the house I know what to tell him," her mother went on after a silence, "I brought all of you through this war. I am not giving in now."

Her grandmother got up and left the room. Ruth started

to gather up the dishes.

"I haven't finished yet," her mother said. Ruth stopped picking up the plates. Her mother sipped the rest of her coffee in slow motion, then put down the cup in a dramatic manner, making a big noise. They got up. Her sister's school had not yet started again and she knew the school building was still an overcrowded military hospital. She could see this was going to be an awful day. Her sister would watch her all the time, then report critically to her mother on what she was doing and wait for her mother to agree.

She was wrong. The day turned out to be an exciting one. Shortly after lunch two English soldiers arrived in a jeep and spoke to her mother, smiling in a friendly way. Their voices sounded very clear and they spoke slowly word after word. She noticed that her mother seemed to understand the English sentences but had to search long and hard for the words to answer. Then her mother accompanied the English men walking around the house.

"Your mother is brazen enough to get through this," her grandmother said, watching the party with her sister, her little brother and herself from the terrace door in the sitting room, "it looks like we're in no danger."

As her grandmother went on talking to them it occurred to her how different her mother and her mother's mother were. One made her anxious and troubled, the other... She could not find a name for her feelings. But she could say that she loved her, yes, she really did. Her grandmother took notice of her, listened to her and sometimes even put an arm around her.

"Those men won't confiscate this house," her grandmother went on calmly, "look, it has no bathroom, no flushing toilet and everybody has to carry water from the pump, in summer and winter, in snow and ice. We'll be staying here till we get permission to go home. The war is not yet over officially. But we are prisoners now. Still, that is not going to stop us having some fun. Let's go."

Her grandmother led them to the boat house where her mother and Ruth were talking to the two English soldiers. Both soldiers looked at Ruth, one said something. Ruth shook her head. She noticed Ruth was wearing her pretty cotton dress and looked lovely as always. The Englishmen smiled at her nanny in silence for a while. Her mother seemed to be impatient with this.

As the silence continued, her mother said almost bossily: "All right then? We ...stay?"

One of the soldiers turned and pointed to the boat house. "Boat?" he asked.

"Yes, boat." Her mother nodded.

It was obvious to her that the soldier wanted to see the boat. He took a few steps in the direction of the boat house, stopped and looked back at her mother. Her mother suddenly started but did not move. Her grandmother took a deep breath and gripped her hand. At this moment Ruth made a gesture to the English soldier near her to indicate that they needed a key to open the door of the boat house. Then Ruth opened her hands, shrugged and made a funny face and she knew at once Ruth was telling the soldiers that the key was lost.

The soldier near the boat house came back. He started telling her mother something. He spoke fast and impatiently. As she looked at her mother's face she registered clearly that her mother was not understanding the meaning of the words. It was a real surprise to her to discover that her mother was at a loss.

Some seconds passed and it seemed to her that time was standing still. Her little brother looked from one of them to the other, puzzling, her sister appeared to be counting the leaves on the Big Tree. Just then her grandmother, with a note of desperation sounding in her voice, said: "Let me handle this" and started to speak in fluent English. Everyone stood watching and listening in disbelief. Even her mother seemed to come to life again.

The two soldiers nodded and the one who had stepped towards the boathouse answered in a friendly manner. He had taken off his cap and she noticed that he kneaded it between his fingers in a nervous manner just as the handyman at the neighbours' hotel wrung his hands when he was talking to his boss.

"What does he want?" her mother hastily asked her grandmother as soon as the soldier stopped talking.

"Wait." Her grandmother ordered, bowed towards the English soldiers and said: "Thank you, thank you so much" and some more words in the foreign language.

"Tell me!" Her mother pressed.

"Wait," her grandmother repeated and again bowed to the soldiers as they were leaving without any further word.

"Now what?" Her mother's face showed no fear anymore. "Tell me. I never knew you could speak English."

Her grandmother seemed not to take offence and announced with amusement: "They are coming back tomorrow afternoon, my dear. You will have to have the key for them then."

She inwardly congratulated her grandmother and discerned triumph in the eyes of the old woman. Her grandmother went on: "Instead of staring at me you should think about how to get rid of your Nazi stuff in there by tomorrow."

As her eyes followed her grandmother's outstretched arm she understood with a glance at the boathouse what was the matter. Her father's books were still drying in there. Those books could tell the same story as her father's coat and pistols would have done before they had been despatched to the bottom of the lake.

————

Refugees in the Night 1945

That night she woke up. Thinking of the key to the boathouse kept her awake for a while. Shortly after the visit of the English soldiers she had discovered that the key really was lost and her mother had been looking for it all afternoon. Her little brother and she had looked everywhere as well. Finally her mother had gone upstairs to ask Frau Mattes if there was a second one. She had followed her mother and noticed that her mother said: "All right." Her mother did not exclaim cheerfully 'Thank you for your help' as she would have expected her to do. Naturally she would have liked to stay upstairs a bit longer but she had the feeling they were not welcome. Frau Mattes' eyes looked red and Herr Mattes shouted from the room into the hallway: "The war is over now. The Nazis have lost. Go home!"

She lay in the darkness for a while, motionless. Her sister and brother were asleep. She could hear their regular breathing. Suddenly she thought she heard a knock at the front door which was just outside her room. And then, yes, there was a knock at the door again. And then a voice called "Halloo!" in an urgent tone. No, it was more a pleading tone. "Halloo! Halloo!" And more knocking.

She got up. She felt the cold floor under her feet and a much colder draft was coming in from the open window and creeping up under her night dress. She opened the door of her bedroom just as her mother was opening the front door. Her mother was wearing a bath robe and had bare feet too.

"Sorry! We are so sorry!" That was a man's voice.

"Someone told us Germans are living here."

"Can we come in?" This was a different voice. It sounded like a boy speaking.

Her mother opened the door wide and in a startling voice almost cried: "Oh, yes, come in! German soldiers are always welcome in this house."

A light was switched on. Two men in German uniforms stepped into the hall. They looked dirty. The uniform of the small soldier seemed wet through. They weren't carrying anything.

"You poor fellows!" Her mother now lowered her voice. "You have found the shelter you need. This is the home of a Waffen SS family. You are so welcome."

Now, with a quick, short movement of the head, her mother caught sight of her at the bedroom door. "What are you doing here?" Her mother's voice sounded full of hate. "Shut the door. Go back to sleep. Immediately."

She retreated. She closed the door. She felt cold. As she passed her sister's bed her sister asked: "What's going on?"

"Nothing," she answered and sat down on her bed.

"So, why are you waking me?" her sister asked, yawning.

She did not respond. She crept under the duvet and tried to stop shivering. She hoped her sister would not hear the voices that now disappeared into the back of the house. After a while it seemed her sister was asleep again. She relaxed. She felt almost happy. She had experienced something and her sister had not. Not long after this exultant thought the bedroom door opened. In the light of the hall lamp she saw the figure of her mother coming in. Her mother went to the wardrobe, took out some things hastily and hung them over her left arm. Then her mother bent down and put her hand to where the shoes were kept. Having evidently found the right pairs - she thought it was two pairs - her mother closed the wardrobe and tiptoed out of the room.

Now she knew what was going on. To make sure she was right she kept herself awake till she heard the front door open again. The young soldier whispered something she could not understand. The other spoke enthusiastically, much louder: "Thank you so much for everything."

Her mother whispered something back, then she heard the door closing. She concentrated intently and forced herself to compose a picture in her mind: Two men in her father's civilian clothes and shoes walking along roads and through fields, jumping over fences and rivers and climbing up hills, always in the direction they imagined Germany to be, always trying to avoid being seen by English troops. Her grandmother had said that some of these fleeing men would succeed in reaching their homeland by hiding in the mountains by day and walking during the night. Some would be taken prisoner.

———

Smoke Signals 1945

She woke up late the next morning. Her sister was just leaving the bedroom, her little brother was sitting in his bed with a picture book, the only children's book in the house. She was astonished to see that her mother's bed was empty. That was unusual. Her mother never got up early. And there was an unusual smell too. Pancakes, she thought, someone is making pancakes. She got out of bed and went into the hall. The kitchen door was open, the smell increased with each step she took towards it.

"Come in! Sit down! Have a pancake," her grandmother said with the particular smile she loved. "No, first call your brother. There will be only the four of us for a feast. Your mother, with poor Ruth helping her, is working hard outside. And don't bother with dressing. It's warm in here. I lit a fire."

As her grandmother was serving up pancakes for her and her little brother and sprinkling sugar over them, her sister said: "Mother won't like it if the little ones are not dressed."

"Your mother has more important things on her mind just now," her grandmother answered as she turned to the stove again. "Enjoy your pancakes. You can have more. There is no bread in the house. It disappeared over night."

"Did the soldiers get it?" She had come to the kitchen with the best of intentions not to mention what she had heard and seen last night. But it was too late now. She had given the game away.

"Soldiers?" Her sister put her knife and fork down and sat

motionless with a puzzled expression on her face.

"My feet are cold," her little brother said, can I kneel on my chair?"

"Of course you can, my boy." She had the impression her grandmother had not heard her words. Her grandmother stirred the rest of the pancake mixture very vigorously.

"I want to know what soldiers you are talking about," her sister demanded, still not eating.

Now her grandmother took a break from her cooking, sat down at the table and in a calm voice explained: "You know the war is over. The soldiers want to go home. But only the ones from the country that did not start the war are allowed do so. German soldiers first have to help rebuild what they destroyed in the occupied countries. If only they could bring back the dead as well."

This explanation reminded her again of her inability to comprehend why there had been a war at all.

"But why is SHE talking about soldiers." Her sister pointed at her.

Her grandmother kept calm. "I imagine she heard the fellows who came last night. They are on their way to Germany. They're hoping to avoid being imprisoned by our liberators. They walked all the way from Italy to Pörtschach. They were hungry. They were tired. I fed them. Your mother gave them civilian clothing. But when I told them that an Austrian couple is living on the second floor they left at once."

"How did they find us?" her sister, who had started work on her pancake, now asked.

"They said a farmer told them because he loved Hitler. Not all Austrians pretend they were against the Nazis."

"I didn't hear them come," her sister said, "why didn't mother wake me?"

Her grandmother shook her head in silence.

"Did they start the fire then?" her little brother asked.

"Which fire?" Now her sister looked quite excited. And confused too.

"Ruth and mother are at it now," her little brother reported, "but there is more smoke than fire. Can I join them after my third pancake, grandma?"

She dressed as quickly as possible. Ruth wasn't there to do her hair properly so she made herself a ponytail and went outside. When she reached the smoking heap she started to cough.

"Stay away," her mother shouted, " I've already sent your brother and sister in again. We've got enough trouble with this business. We don't need children around on top of everything else."

She did not go back into the house. She used the Big Tree as a hiding place. Her mother seemed not to notice. Her mother was complaining that it was the books that were causing all the trouble. "Those fellows' uniforms will burn better," Ruth was informed, "they are dirty but, thank God, they dried overnight. Get the jackets. The fire needs a boost. And the trousers are not so dangerous anyway."

Minutes passed. The flames rose, the smoke as well. She was just thinking about what kind of danger her mother meant when she heard a jeep coming. Then she saw it slowly rolling down the drive.

"There they are already. Goodness me!" Her mother's voice was full of surprise and fear. "They said they would come in the afternoon. You see there is no relying on them."

Now the thought occurred to her that she was watching a story. There was the picture of the fire with a column of white smoke rising high into the air. There were two women moving nervously around and poking at things that then vanished in flames. In this scene there now appeared two men who were not supposed to come into the story yet at all. They were to come later, after the fire had burnt down, to have a look at the boathouse.

She could not stop herself thinking that she was telling herself an amazing story, especially when she suddenly noticed that the two English soldiers were not the men from the day before. These soldiers were officers. She saw the different caps and the many coloured decorations on their uniform jackets. They did not look like they were only coming to inspect a boathouse. She thought they looked strong and powerful as she watched them marching straight towards the fire. Powerful and determined. Her mother seemed to have the same impression. Her mother straightened up and made Ruth do so too. Just then the flames caught hold of the rest of the clothes and books, blazed into a furious confusion of colours and then fell back under a new outburst of smoke.

"Are you sending smoke signals?" one of the officers asked in perfect German, in a voice that carried far. "Nothing will come of it. We got all your men."

Her mother did not answer. Neither did Ruth. But Ruth never said much anyway. The English walked around the fire. The one who had spoken before asked: "What were you burning?"

She could see her mother shrugged.

"Tell me!" the officer ordered.

Next she heard her mother's loud voice stammer: "We cannot take everything back with us to Germany. You should know that."

The officer touched his comrade's arm and turned towards the drive. Both took a few steps, than the second English man turned back to shout in German: "You are not leaving. You stay!" And after a short pause went on in the same strong voice: "We shall tell you when you have to leave."

She realised the story had reached its end. She was not sure if she was happy about it or not. She still did not know when she would have to say good bye to the lake and if she would start school here or somewhere else. As she was thinking this she remembered her grandmother saying: "I want to go home. I miss my brothers and sisters. I want to go soon." Her grandmother would be unhappy about the delay. But probably her mother would not tell her grandmother what had happened by the fire. Her mother mostly talked about things that had turned out well thanks to her own involvement.

That day in the afternoon her sister went to see a friend. As she watched her sister leave, walking beside her grandmother and not taking the bicycle, it occurred to her that this was actually going to be a special day. She planned to cycle around the grounds until her sister appeared again. The only interruption would be the soldiers coming to see the boathouse. But the boathouse was ready to be seen. Her mother had said earlier: "They may look around as long as they want to now. They will not find anything hidden anymore. I did a good job."

Her joy did not last long. The moment the jeep came down the drive and she noticed Frau Mattes standing on the balcony in front of their room she had an uneasy feeling. She leant the bicycle against the house and sat down on the first step of the stairs which led to the front door. Her mother came out and, thank God, did not say anything about the bicycle. Her mother went straight to the jeep, smiling broadly, stretching out a hand to welcome the visitors. She noticed that the soldiers did not even look at the hand. They went straight to the boathouse. Her mother followed them, now not smiling anymore. The three of them disappeared into the boathouse. After a while her mother came out again, walked towards the house, past her, hurried up the stairs and into the hall without a single word. The front door shut with a loud bang.

Feeling a little concerned about Frau Mattes, she looked up to the balcony. Frau Mattes was still standing there. They smiled at each other. But it was a worrying smile. Just at that moment the garage-like double doors on the lake side of the boathouse opened and the boat came into view. One of the soldiers was rowing. She saw the other one leaving the boathouse. He went straight back to the jeep, waved at his comrade and drove off. By now his comrade was rowing far out on the lake. After a while he changed direction. The turn would bring him to the harbour in Pörtschach, she thought. The English would keep the boat.

As she became aware of this she looked up to Frau Mattes again. Frau Mattes was gazing after the rowing soldier. And the beautiful boat. She herself had been very fond of the boat. Her place had been in the stern with her brother. Once her mother had deciphered two letters, an A and an L, cast in the iron railing around the wide seat. But they never asked Herr and Frau Mattes what the letters stood for.

Now Frau Mattes took a handkerchief out of her pocket and dried first one eye and then the other in slow motion.

"Are you sad?" she heard herself asking upwards. She regretted her words immediately.

But Frau Mattes seemed not to be offended. Frau Mattes put her handkerchief back, leant down to her and answered in a friendly manner: "The boat was a present from my husband when we first married. He welded those letters himself into the railing. They are the initial letters of my maiden name."

While she was still thinking of something nice to say to Frau Mattes, something that was really comforting, Frau Mattes left the balcony and closed the door of their room.

———

Lettuce 1945

She was hungry all the time. When the war was still on she had always left the dining room hungry. Three times a day. Now the war was over but she still felt the hunger all day. Her mother went to Pörtschach every morning, but came home with hardly any purchases. Bread, butter, meat and all those things were rationed. Sometimes not available at all. Often her mother complained about the shop owner: "He says it's all gone when I just saw someone leaving with a loaf of bread." She saw that her mother was full of anger. "He is punishing us because we were Nazis. But it was not my doing that everything ended like this."

Her grandmother never replied. Ruth was mostly too busy to listen to her mother's laments.

"Go and ask Alwina for some carrots and a lettuce," her mother said one morning to her sister. When she heard this, she knew straightaway it would be she who would end up going to the allotment where Alwina grew vegetables between the hotel and the Villa Caprice. Alwina worked in the hotel and looked after the potatoes and cabbage and strawberries as well. She liked talking to her. Alwina always wore a scarf and was very kind and sometimes stopped digging and stretched and addressed a few friendly words to her while she was sitting in the grass near the garden gate. Sometimes she got some vegetables to bring to her mother.

She knew getting something as a present was all right as long as you said 'Thank you very much' in a friendly way. But her grandmother had once told her that asking for something was an unfriendly thing to do and unpleasant for the other person.

There it was already. "I am not going," her sister said. Her sister wasn't back at school yet and was impatiently waiting for the new start. "Send her. They always chat."

Naturally she wanted to show that she wasn't keen to go either. But she knew there was no escape. Her mother would blame her again for letting the whole family starve. Her mother had done that before. An English soldier had once offered to bring her into the kitchen of the hotel where he was going to order some food so that she would have something to bring to her family. She didn't like the man. She refused. When she was telling Ruth about the incident her mother listened and afterwards reproached her for being selfish.

Alwina was digging out potatoes. At the garden gate she noticed one big basket filled to the brim with early 'soil apples', as the Austrians called potatoes. Jockl, the old farmhand, would collect the basket later with a wheelbarrow.

"Hello," Alwina said as she approached the fence, "how are you today, my girl?" But Alwina was not looking at her. More and more potatoes went into the second basket. "I haven't seen you around for a while."

"We've been swimming a lot, " she answered, happy not to have to talk about the real topic straightaway. "I taught my brother how to swim properly. He was only able to dive. But he was very good at that."

"That's odd," Alwina answered.

"The English took Herr and Frau Mattes' boat," she went on.

"I know." Alwina got up. "But I'm sure they will give it back as soon as you are gone."

She was confused now about where their conversation had led. The truth was, she told herself, she felt utterly lost. How could she start to explain that she had been sent to ask for something from the garden? She felt a mixture of both fear and relief when she decided not to beg. She stepped back from the fence. At just that moment Alwina bent down again, took some potatoes from the basket and asked: "Want some?"

She simply nodded.

"Wait! I'll put you some in a bag." Alwina seemed eager to please her. "And you can have some cabbage and lettuce as well. Won't that be nice?"

Again she only nodded. She felt a strong urge to hug Alwina. But there was still a distance between them. She knew that just a second later she would be too shy to do it.

———

Love 1945

"What's going on over there?" Her mother was listening to the noise of trucks driving into the hotel yard one morning. They were all listening. Only her sister was missing from the kitchen. School had started again.

"There are new troops coming," Ruth said.

"Have the others gone already?"

"Yes. The English aren't using the hotel for a holiday anymore. Now they're using it to assemble the troops that will be sent home." Ruth was washing the dishes, her grandmother drying.

Her mother finished combing her little brother's hair. "How do you know?"

"My friend told me. She lost her boyfriend weeks ago. He should be back with his family by now." Ruth bent deeper over the water bowl. "He promised to write. As soon as he got home. But he didn't."

"She was going out with an English soldier?" Her mother seemed astonished. Her little brother who had just tied up his shoe laces asked: "Can I go now ?"

"Wait," her mother ordered.

"She loved him." Ruth rattled a saucepan.

"If you're talking about Maria, the girl with the plain face, how would she know anything about love?"

Ruth turned and looked at her mother and answered: "Maria knows what love is. She is my age. She's very sad."

She heard these defiant words and knew that Ruth must

be thinking of Heinrich. Heinrich was dead, but Ruth had loved him. Then suddenly it struck her that her mother must be thinking of her father now. Her father was gone too, he was dead, would not be coming back. Her mother had certainly loved him.

"Do you miss father?" she heard herself asking her mother. The boldness of this question made her shiver. Of course her mother missed her father. Like Ruth missed Heinrich and like Maria was now missing the English boyfriend. No, with Maria it was different. The boyfriend was at home, it was possible for him to write or come back. Her father and Heinrich couldn't do anything like that. They were gone forever.

She thought this as she waited anxiously for her mother to answer her dangerous question, hoping that she might somehow still avoid getting into trouble.

"I must admit I don't know the answer to that." Her mother pushed her little brother towards the door, indicating that he should leave the kitchen. He did so. She heard him even leaving the house. Her mother paid no attention to this but folded her arms and looked at the ceiling: "It was different with him when he was here that last time. A war makes men rough. I don't actually know how we would have got on if he had come back."

She saw no sign of emotion in her mother.

"We would have been fine, Heinrich and me." In haste, Ruth handed the last plate to her grandmother, took the bucket and said to her: "Come on, we'll get some water."

She was disappointed as she left the kitchen with Ruth. She had hoped they would go on talking about her father. Her mother seldom mentioned him. The last her mother had said was that her father should have been a bit more careful at the front and not let his wife become a widow with three children. Ruth often told her things about Heinrich, sometimes with tears in her eyes. Then she too cried a bit with Ruth.

The day had not started very pleasantly, and it got worse. Her little brother, who had gone to see the trucks at the hotel and give them a full inspection as he liked to do, was brought home with a broken leg. He had been amusing himself talking to the troops that were newly arrived and kindly offering to show them around. Then he had evidently hung on to a truck as it was leaving and fallen off when the vehicle stopped at the end of the drive. Her mother accused her of not having done her job. It should have been her duty to look after her brother since her sister was back at school.

She was not allowed to accompany her mother when she took the young patient to the hospital in Klagenfurt, although the English driver of the car offered to look after her.

The party was back sooner than she had expected. By listening in to what was said, she gathered that there had been no plaster in the hospital. Her mother had got her son bandaged and had to take him home again. The English driver merely shrugged and left her mother standing there, outraged about the whole wicked world.

It was her grandmother, with her talent for practical advice, who said: "My dear daughter, wouldn't it be easy enough for you to use your charm to get help in your enemies' hospital?"

This made her fear a new round of arguments. But that was not going to happen. No sooner had her grandmother said the word 'hospital' than her mother went off again only to return a short while later, beaming with delight and bearing the news that an English doctor was to come the next day to fix her brother's leg.

A friendly team of two from the military hospital in Pörtschach arrived the next morning and she watched them happily as they tended her little brother on the dining table. When the doctor and his assistant left, the doctor advised her mother to bring her little brother in to them again a few days later. They would be able to fix something like a stirrup to her little brother's plastered foot, he said, so that the sweet little fellow would be able to start his adventures all over again.

Nor was she permitted to accompany them when the plaster had hardened and her mother got the loan of a wheelbarrow to bring the patient for his further treatment.

"I have to give my attention to the boy," her mother said as she asked to be allowed to walk with them to Pörtschach, "and who will look after you there among all those soldiers?"

That evening, as she was on her way to say good night to her mother and grandmother and her sister was still proudly reading a baby story to her brother, she heard her mother say: "I am astonished that the doctor has done this for me. That the English gave me help so willingly. We have been enemies for so long and now..."

"They did it for your poor little son who's not even five yet." Her grandmother's voice was clear, not at all reproachful . "Your little boy isn't responsible for what we have done to them."

———

An Accident 1945

Naturally it never entered her head that it would be the last time ever that she would sit with her sister and play cards with her little brother. It was the last day of the summer holidays for those who were already at school. Her big event was to come later in the month. That morning her sister had reluctantly agreed to join in their game till it was time for her to leave to see a friend.

"Georgina is meeting me at eleven at the hotel," her sister said and went on in a superior tone of voice: "Listen, you little ones: Mother has given me permission to walk into the village to see the fair."

"We shall go later on too!" her little brother answered.

"No you won't, my dear." Her sister handed out the cards. "Mother is sorting out the wardrobes and Ruth has to help her. And you are not old enough anyway."

She would have liked to go to the fair as well. With Georgina. Georgina was nice but never stayed in their house for long. Her mother did not like Georgina. "That girl never looks at me," her mother had complained once. "And she gives very short, impolite answers. She should have more respect."

Her grandmother had told her what respect meant and, since then, whenever she met Herr and Frau Mattes she tried to show them a lot of respect. She always answered with whole sentences and tried to meet the eyes of her friends. Herr Mattes once said: "You are not the daughter of that woman. You can't be, my girl." But that was a joke. Herr Mattes often joked and then

Frau Mattes laughed and seemed very happy.

She liked playing cards. To have company and be passing the time was what she liked. Not the excitement of winning or losing. And it was a fine day. The sun was shining, the lake was calm, the right weather to go and sit out on the island. Often the wind was too strong to use the table and the two benches there. Herr Mattes had told her that he made the bridge to his retreat himself. He had used a large bridge in a foreign country as a model. That big bridge could carry cars and was very long, but now it had been destroyed by the war. Herr Mattes' bridge was only five paces long and had one carved railing.

It was the first time her little brother was able to understand fully what they were doing and he was happy and made funny remarks when he scored a point. She was simply enjoying the company and didn't like it when, every now and then, her sister shouted back to the house: "What time is it, mother?"

After a while, when there was still loads of time to go, Ruth called over that it was nearly time for the meeting. Her sister got very upset and ran from the island cursing loudly and leaving her little brother almost in tears.

She was engrossed in her effort to keep up a simple made-up game with her little brother and did not really notice that, just after her sister left, there was suddenly rushing about and shouting in the house. It was only when Ruth came and stood at the other end of the bridge, her face strange and rigid, that it occurred to her something unusual was going on. She put the cards down, got up, told her little brother to wait a minute and went to meet Ruth in the middle of the bridge.

"There's been an accident," Ruth said , "your sister has

been injured. Your mother has just gone on her bicycle to be with her at Dr Harder's surgery."

"Then she will be brought to my hospital," her little brother shouted from where he was still sitting.

Ruth looked at the boy tenderly. "She will indeed. There was a truck involved. Like in your case. Let's stay calm and wait."

They had to wait a long time. Her grandmother made pancakes at lunchtime but they did not eat a lot. There was no news. The hands of the clock in the dining room moved on to three, four, five and further and there was no news and her mother did not come back either.

Her mother came late in the evening. She saw immediately that something terrible had happened. Her mother looked like she had been crying for hours.

"Does it look bad?" her grandmother asked softly, having sat her mother down in the armchair beside the dining table. They all stared at her mother.

"She has died. She is dead!" Her mother's voice was quiet and small.

Her grandmother held on to her mother's shoulders. Nobody spoke. She did not know what to think. The four of them, her grandmother, Ruth, her little brother and she, all suddenly seemed like immovable figures standing around her mother.

"Bring the children out," her mother said after what seemed like ages, "I'll tell you then."

Her grandmother and Ruth did not move. Neither did she or her little brother.

"Go!" her mother said in a stronger voice addressing her and her little brother and shaking her hand as if to push something away. "This is not for you."

She learned later that her sister was struck by an English lorry, driven by a German prisoner. Her sister was so badly injured that her system could not survive it. Her grandmother said that in her little brother's hospital in Klagenfurt they had done all they could to save the girl's life. It had been very moving to see how hard they tried. And all the time the driver of the truck had sat in the waiting room and cried his eyes out. He kept saying over and over that her sister's attention must have been focussed entirely on the girl on the other side on the road. She had run straight out into him.

Once she plucked up enough courage to ask her mother to tell her more about her sister. Had they said anything to each other in the hospital? And what else had...? But her mother shook her head and said: "Leave me alone. Don't make things worse. Can't you see I am at the end of my tether?"

———

Funeral **1945**

For several days she did not know where to be, where to go, what to do. She did not miss her sister that much, not yet, but life at home had changed and she was afraid about who would be next, who would be the next one to die.

Her mother stayed in bed in the sitting room where they had put the bed so that she and her little brother couldn't bother her. Finally, one lunchtime, her grandmother announced that her mother was ready to join them at the table again. But her mother did not show up and Ruth had to bring her a small slice of bread and the usual coffee.

"It's not right," her grandmother said, "your mother should try at least. This war was started by a certain party after all and thousands and thousands of mothers have had to cope with loss."

"But she really does feel ill," Ruth answered, "I'll take the kids to Pörtschach later. Anni in the shop promised me some eggs and flour. Only her parents mustn't find out."

Looking forward to going into the village reminded her that she was to start school soon. But when? There was nothing prepared for her. She remembered very well the first day her sister went to school back in the Warthegau. How exciting it had been then. She recalled perfectly the night her mother could not sleep because it had been impossible to get all the things that were needed for someone starting school. When you started school, she remembered, you had to have something to write on and naturally something to write with and you needed a satchel and a dress that had been washed and ironed for the occasion. And, very important, there had to be a sweets bag filled with chocolate and apples and the like. In Poland her mother had startled everyone in the Big House with complaints about the lack of sweets. Here, now, what was worrying her most of all was: After her sister died nobody even mentioned that she too was due to start school.

Next day her mother was sent notice that her sister's body had been brought back to Pörtschach to be buried. "They dare to choose the date!" her mother cried, reading the letter aloud to Ruth and her grandmother. "Shouldn't it be my choice? When I am ready?"

Frau Gruber came to ask when the funeral would take place and, in a friendly manner, explained that the neighbours had sent her to find out.

"It's a private event only," her mother let Frau Gruber know, "only myself, my mother and Ruth are going."

"And the children, naturally," Frau Gruber said, looking at her.

"No. They are staying." Her mother shook her head, absolutely determined.

Frau Gruber left after that and she went with her. Frau Gruber gave her a cup of Ersatz coffee and a slice of fresh baked bread and told her that Fritzi had been watching the chef at the hotel and then taken a piece of dough that had been thrown away in a bin. Frau Gruber had baked it at once and it should taste really good. She could tell straightaway: Yes, the bread was delicious. And the coffee better than ever.

"So, my girl, are you missing your sister? Are you very sad? First your father and now…"

She heard herself answering promptly: "It's not me, Frau Gruber, it's my mother who is suffering. Because my mother has lost a child. And that is very bad."

Frau Gruber stayed quiet for a moment and she began to fear she had been impertinent when finally Frau Gruber's expression changed. Frau Gruber looked really caring now as she asked: "How old are you, my girl? Six and a bit now, aren't you?"

She nodded. She knew she should not have corrected the nice neighbour. She should not have said what she just said. But it was the truth. It had become clear to her that in her house the only one who had the right to be sad was her mother.

The morning before the funeral her mother asked if she and her little brother wanted to stay in the house or go outside while the adults were away. "Because we have to lock the doors," her mother said.

"Outside," she said. It was a lovely day, very warm, with no wind and so no waves on the water.

"Here in the house," her little brother said.

Her mother didn't seem to care about resolving this difference, but only said nervously: "Sort it out yourselves. We are leaving in half an hour."

It did not take long to get her little brother to agree to her wishes. She promised to tell him a story, maybe even two, or however many it would take while they waited outside under the Big Tree. In any case, Frau Gruber had offered to look after them. But Frau Gruber would not be able to do that if they were locked in.

The sun crossed well over to the right and was already shining on the rose bed but the three of them were not back yet. Frau Gruber needed some help at the pump and Frau Mattes asked her to pick some dog daisies and said thank you with a plate of cheese sandwiches. But this did not help to pass the time very well. Just when she was beginning to feel forgotten and abandoned and her little brother was crying quietly, she realized she had better do something because probably there had been another accident, she heard her mother's loud voice coming nearer. She must have been quite sunk in her brooding for she was startled by this. Her little brother was already running up the drive shouting: "They are back, Frau Gruber!"

As she stood under the Big Tree and watched and listened she told herself she could try later to work out what had happened at the funeral. To her surprise Herr and Frau Mattes came out of the house as soon as her mother, her grandmother and Ruth reached the Big Tree. Herr Mattes was carrying a small container with white flowers. So was Frau Gruber who stretched out a hand to her mother and said: "We wanted to give you something to put on the grave." Frau Mattes asked: "Did the priest's words help to give you strength?"

"There was no priest. I did not need a priest." The words reminded her again how different her mother was from other women.

"There was only the undertaker," her mother explained, "and he was no help at all. I asked him to come and tend the grave again in a few weeks. And do you know what he had the audacity to reply? He said: 'If you give me a pair of shoes as payment I'll do it. Money is useless now.' Yes, that's what he said to a mother in mourning at the grave of her daughter."

"His name is Robert!" They all looked at Ruth. Ruth lowered her head but went on in a firm voice: "He lost his two sons last year at the front and his wife is not well and there have been so many German soldiers dying at the school hospital. He had to be treated there himself for a while. My friend's mother looks after his two smaller girls. He is very good to her."

Afterwards she remembered how her mother had been unable to respond to Ruth's words but went straight into the house. The other women did not say much either. Her grandmother stayed till they all had gone, then took her and her little brother's hand and said: "Let's be brave now. That's the only thing we can do."

———

School **1945**

When she could stand the uncertainty no longer she asked Ruth to find out when school would start. "In three days," Ruth reported after coming back from shopping on her mother's bike. "It took them so long to renovate your classroom. And they had no paint for the walls. A teacher told me the whole school looked awful after the wounded men had been moved out."

Later that day, after her grandmother had performed the miracle of serving up a big bowl of potatoes and a piece of fried fish for everyone, she saw her mother leaving the house. After a while she spotted her at the boathouse and went to meet her. Her mother walked on as she approached her. She stayed at her mother's side. They did not talk. Her mother walked into the wood. But she was impatient now to hear what her mother thought about the school problem.

"Can I have her satchel?" she forced herself to ask. "School is starting in three days, on Thursday." Naturally it would be lost on her mother how well she knew the days of the week. She had known them for ages and was able to count them forwards and backwards for a whole month. And she should have made some reference to her sister. But she could not bring herself to do so.

Her mother went on in silence.

"May I?" What she felt now, above all, was fear.

Her mother said nothing.

In her mind she told herself to be more direct. "Nothing is ready for my first day," she said. It startled her that she really had spoken this sentence.

"How dare you!" Her mother stopped walking, looked at her angrily, and went on.

She let her go. She had the depressing feeling she had hurt her mother deeply.

It was her grandmother who packed the satchel for her. "Of course you may have it and also your sister's books and the slate if you promise to look after it well," her grandmother said that afternoon.

Ruth promised to accompany her to school.

"The teachers will know that I am unable to attend," her mother said during breakfast on her big day. "After this war things are not what they were before. Thank God the Austrians are not so keen on bringing sweet bags for the start of school. We wouldn't have anything to put in one anyway, would we?"

School was a big surprise to her. She couldn't get over the fact that people she had never known were interested in what she was thinking, what she knew and what she wanted. She liked her teacher from the first second. Nobody talked about her being the child of a German SS family. All she heard, while Ruth was signing some papers, was the mother of the nice boy who was to sit beside her saying: "Children are not to blame."

She went home alone. As she walked between the fields and orchards, along the narrow pathway which ran parallel to the main road and the railway line, it began to occur to her that she had started a new life. A better one, of course. And that she was determined to enjoy it.

———

Farmer Franz 1945

She never found out where her mother had first met Farmer Franz. But whenever her mother needed help, the sort of help her mother could not get from anyone else, it was Farmer Franz, from far up in the mountains, who would be asked. It was he who took their dog when there was no more food for the friendly bitch, and when fresh butter suddenly appeared on the breakfast table that was from him too.

She was sure lack of food was not the only reason her mother had got rid of the dog. 'Witchy' was unexpectedly pregnant and her mother said this would mean a lot of trouble.

She had loved the dog, a spaniel they had got shortly before her father stayed with them. Her father loved the dog as well. It had always kept her company and let her stroke it whenever she liked. When her mother had first turned up with Witchy she had said it was a surprise gift for the whole family. But in the end her mother took her decision 'unilaterally', as her grandmother called it. For a long time after the dog was gone she wanted to tell her mother that it had not been fair to give them something and then take it away again. But of course she never said anything like this. Her little brother once said "father would have kept Witchy". She agreed.

She and her little brother were afraid of Farmer Franz. She could not tell why exactly. There was something in his eyes she did not like, the way he looked. And she disliked his manner of pronouncing so many strange words in the Austrian accent. He let his grey hair grow long and he did not have a wife. One of his many farmhands did the cooking, her mother said. But badly, her mother added.

One afternoon she had to accompany her mother to the farm. Her mother didn't let her do her homework first. Her mother did not want to go on her own because it was a hard boring slog, uphill all the time. When they got to the farm her mother went into the house. She had to stay outside. She sat and waited in front of a shed and, at first, chatted to all the men who passed by. She asked where her dog was. "Gone," a man said. Eventually the yard emptied and she got terribly bored. She walked around the farm. In one building some men were milking cows. One gave her a mug of lukewarm milk and said: "You better stay at home the next time."

At last her mother arrived out in the doorway of the farmhouse and shouted something back into the hall. Her voice sounded excited and at the same time charming and amused. She felt relieved. They were to go home now. She was hungry and still thirsty. Her mother walked fast and did not talk. But she had to accept that. Life was, she had come so see, split into two parts. There was a part for adults and there was one for children. The adults were allowed to interfere in the children's part. But children had no influence. In most events children were not even allowed to take part.

Absorbed as she was in her thoughts, it took her by surprise that her mother suddenly looked at her and asked: "Are you all right?"

The question made her feel an awful weakness. She hesitated for a while before answering: "I waited a long time."

Her mother looked straight ahead again but she could see her mother's face brightening. "Sorry, I had to talk to him.

We really need firewood. He promised some. Ruth and I will have to do a lot of sawing, it's true. But at least we can go on cooking and if we stay the winter..."

"Witchy is gone," she said.

"I know."

"Where is she?"

"I didn't ask. Don't fret about it. It makes me nervous." Her mother's voice sounded reproachful now as it so often did.

They went on downhill. She felt more tired. It seemed to her that walking beside her mother was not different from watching the unfamiliar men milking the cows. The fact was she did not belong.

———

Firewood 1945

The day the firewood arrived she came home from school late. There had been a meeting to discuss the Christmas party. Her class was chosen to sing a Christmas song while everyone was sitting down for their coffee and cake. She had never been to a big gathering, a party or similar occasion, and she was looking forward to seeing what it was like. She imagined there must be a special atmosphere to the whole thing.

Ruth had kept her lunch on the stove. It seemed to her the house was unusually quiet. She asked Ruth, who was doing the dishes, what was going on.

"It has been an unpleasant morning," Ruth answered without turning round, "your brother ran away, no, actually your mother is saying that he ran away again, that he had been warned once before, and now..."

"Is he back?" she asked and felt the splendour of her own morning fading away.

"Oh, yes." Ruth put the sponge into the washing-up bowl and looked at her saying: "I don't even believe he did actually run away. Your grandmother and he were playing hide and seek and he ran off further and got talking to someone at the hotel and forgot ..."

"That sounds like him," she said smiling and went on eating her mashed potatoes.

"Now your mother is sending him to Farmer Franz. For good! Your mother told him she does not want him here anymore."

When Ruth said this she could not go on eating. She thought it was quite possible her mother had made this dreadful decision. Her mother had often enough moaned about how hard the future would be trying to raise two children as a war widow.

"What are we going to do, Ruth?" she asked. "Where is he now? And where is my grandmother? Do you want me to run to Frau Gruber?"

"He and your grandmother are packing his rucksack." To her surprise she saw Ruth smile now.

But in her anxiety she did not catch on at once. She cried: "The poor boy. He is so afraid of Farmer Franz. Grandmother must..." She calmed herself. "Ruth, tell me what you know."

"Your grandmother has already done what she 'must', my girl."

Ruth sat down on the chair beside her. "Your brother was in tears breaking his heart at lunch and your mother sent him out of the room. Your grandmother followed him saying: I'll help him to pack and winked at me. Your brother had stopped crying by the time he got in the hall!"

"And then what?" she asked and started eating again.

"You will see a real little drama later on. It going to go like this: Your brother will come out of the house with his belongings, still in tears but now pretend ones. Your mother wanted your grandmother to take the boy half-way up the mountains before telling him... you know, what I mean. But your grandmother has told him the truth already. So they will both leave with lots of 'bye-byes' and you had better shed some tears as well. They will come back after a plausible length of time and your brother will promise...you know what I mean."

"It's still not right, though."

"There was no other way your grandmother could contradict. Her nerves have suffered."

"Father would not have liked it." She surprised herself by saying this.

"I am sure he wouldn't." Ruth went back to the dishes.

It was a dreadful performance. Her grandmother and her little brother arrived back late in the afternoon. Her brother recited a sentence he had learned by heart in which he promised never ever to be naughty again. Her mother shed tears and hugged him.

Just as she was thinking of going to see Frau Gruber to tell her about the Christmas song and how they were going to ring bells while they sang, a horse-drawn wagon with a load of tree trunks from Farmer Franz arrived and stopped at the road side. Her mother cried out: "Oh, that man is great. It's here already," and ran up the drive. Halfway up her mother stopped, pointed at her brother and shouted: "You go back into the house and stay there!"

———

Two German Prisoners **1945**

She hurried home from school the next day. Her grandmother had promised to cook noodles and assumed the two female labourers at the firewood pile would want an early lunch. She had noticed that Farmer Franz had sent a strong saw with two handles and a sawhorse as well. All the same, she was expecting her mother to be even more bad-tempered than usual from sawing the timber with Ruth, cursing her unbearable fate as the two of them sweated and groaned among the heavy blocks of wood.

But as she approached the Villa Caprice and heard loud unfamiliar voices, men's voices, and her mother's happy voice in the gaps between, she realised she had imagined it wrong. There was certainly no one there in a bad mood. From the top of the drive she noticed two men in shirts which looked as though they belonged to uniforms. The men were sawing. One big piece of wood was just falling clear. The next followed in no time at all. Then another one. The men were talking and laughing without stopping their sawing for a second. Her mother and Ruth carried the blocks in their arms and she noticed a lot already piled up against the wall beside her bedroom window.

She went down the drive. She heard her mother shouting: "You have restored my faith in miracles!"

One of the men straightened up, pointed at Ruth and answered smiling: "If you want the miracle to go on make sure you keep that girl here."

As she reached the group she saw Ruth had blushed. Now

she knew the two men liked Ruth. Just then her grandmother announced lunch was ready. They all went into the house. The two men said 'Hallo' to her and asked what her name was. Both men had friendly faces. The younger one was limping a bit, and the older one had a deep red scar over his right eye. And a second one on his neck when he opened his shirt. He said: "I'm fine," and briefly put his hand on her head.

Of course her mother did not tell her what had happened that morning. Nor did her grandmother know what had been going on. At long last after they had all had their share of noodles, her mother started to explain the presence of their German guests and talked with such enthusiasm that she knew this would be one of those stories her mother would repeat again and again for everyone who was willing to listen.

"Once we started sawing we actually did not mind the work," her mother said looking at her grandmother, "you know how capable I am of working hard. I was delighted to have the tree-trunks. The load will last till the end of next winter."

"I hope they'll let us leave this country before that," her grandmother remarked. The younger German smiled at Ruth.

"Mother, please!" Her mother's forehead creased sharply and she expected her to say something to her grandmother. But no, her mother went on as though she were telling a fairy story: "As we were sawing hard, all of a sudden an English soldier, a boyish looking one, showed up at the end of the drive with these two men and two more behind him. And straightaway, you, my dear Wolfgang, shouted: 'Germans?' and the four of you came down the drive leaving the English soldier behind you as if he did not belong with you."

"The English soldier was carrying a rifle," her little

brother said.

"I don't believe he even knows how to use it, that young lad," said the older German, whose name was Wolfgang, touching her little brother's hand, "that's how we were able to take such a liberty."

Bit by bit she learned that the German prisoners had been sent to repair a stretch of the road further down in direction of Klagenfurt and that all four prisoners had started work for her mother instead until the English soldier came down the drive too and politely, very politely, invited two of the prisoners to go with him and let the other two stay to help with the sawing.

"How could we let German women do such hard men's work?" Wolfgang asked. "That English fellow could easily start the tarmac cooking himself."

Her grandmother did not laugh with the others. Ruth looked at her plate.

"Can anybody understand how the English managed to win the war?" her mother asked with a contemptuous grin on her face.

The younger German prisoner stopped eating and she saw how he was struck by her mother's words. He looked around the table as if he were sizing everyone up and then remarked: "They did not win the war, Frau Schubert. They liberated us! As you all must surely know."

There was silence for a while and then her mother asked pleasantly about life in a camp and showed astonishment when the prisoners said that the food was good and there was plenty of it and that they did not have to work too hard.

"That's why we're happy to do this job for you," Wolfgang explained and she knew he was joking.

The Germans left when the English soldier and the other two prisoners called in at the Villa Caprice again late in the afternoon. While the English man stood there, apparently admiring the lake, the four prisoners invited her family to a German Christmas party in the camp. Her mother was delighted and said yes, she would be happy to come and see all those brave men and that she was sure it would be a pleasure for the lonely prisoners too to have an officer's wife as their guest.

Wolfgang waved back from the road and shouted: "Ruth, make sure she lets you come."

When the group was out of sight her mother turned to Ruth and said: "Of course you will come too. I don't see why he said that."

"I do!" Her grandmother looked amused as she shouted from the front door: "They saw through you, my dear! I would call that remarkably astute."

———

Christmas **1945**

The preparations for the school Christmas party did not go entirely smoothly. For her. At home. At school it was going well. They practised the song of the little snowdrop every morning and were making great progress. Her problem was the bell. As soon as her teacher asked everyone to bring a little bell, of whatever kind, to the get-together she knew there would an argument with her mother. The bells were needed to accompany a line in the chorus.

"I need a bell for 'Ring, little bell, ring!' she forced herself to say one evening shortly before the event at school.

"Is that a Christmas song?" Ruth asked.

"The Nazis said it was." Her grandmother answered smiling at Ruth. "Times do not change quickly."

"We don't have a bell you could bring," her mother, to her astonishment, did not seem annoyed by this talk.

"You trained the catholic Austrians well," her grandmother went on, "more than seven months have gone by without Nazis and they still don't mention Christ."

Now she felt she had to sort out her problem at once. "Grandma, in some carols we do mention him," she said, nodding broadly to underline her words. Then she looked at her mother: "But for my song I need a bell." As soon as she said it she hoped she hadn't sounded too impatient. She could have said that without a bell she would feel conspicuous. She was an outsider in her class in any case. The only German pupil and, what was more, from an SS family. "There is the big one we only use on

Christmas Eve. May I take that?"

"That's too loud and anyway I don't..." Her mother stopped and looked at her grandmother's hand tapping the table.

"She can take that one. It's better than being without." Her grandmother sounded as though she were giving a special instruction. The headmaster of her school sometimes spoke in that sort of voice. Then, looking at her more gently, added: "You'll have to ring very carefully, with a light touch, my girl, then you'll be fine. And so will your mother. I do appreciate the effort the school makes every year to bring teachers and parents together."

"I am not going. I am not at all anxious to meet all those people. They are going to expel us."

When she heard this it struck her that her mother had never intended to come at all. Her mother had never asked how school was and never listened to her reports about how preparations for the party were going.

"I am going to a ball instead, with Bill, at the English casino." Suddenly her mother's face was glowing. And there was silence. Nobody spoke. The only sound was her little brother's scratching on her slate. She had been kind enough to let him to use it, as long as he was careful, of course.

She thought of Bill. He was a friendly man in an English uniform, with a funny moustache. He sometimes came in the evening to be with her mother. And sometimes her mother went to meet him at his place. Her mother said Bill was a nice man and that it was a miracle to meet such a person. Then her mother would be in a blissful mood and would stay a while by their beds.

"You're going dancing. So, so!" her grandmother said after a while. "But, my dear, your dancing won't start in the afternoon. Don't let her..."

"I decide for myself what I am doing and what not."

These words made her wish she could be catapulted out of the room.

"If I go to the party, I shall be tired in the evening. And I shall look it," her mother went on.

"Your Englishman won't mind it if he loves you."

Her mother got up, as did Ruth. Her mother looked at her grandmother and almost shouted: "Stop it! Not in front of the children! And by the way Bill is actually Scottish."

With some relief she saw her grandmother smiling and heard her say in a meaningful way: "It is the children I am thinking of just now."

Her grandmother put away her knitting needles and addressed her: "Well, my girl, would you like to take me instead of this pretty mother of yours with her prior engagements? I would rather like to go to a Christmas party again."

Later, in bed, she thought that there was more going on between her mother and her grandmother than she was able to understand. But for now she had made sure of a bell and of nice company for the party. She felt utterly relieved and wondered if she had shown enough gratitude to her grandmother when she replied: "I would love to take you, Grandma. There will be the sort of marble cake you like so much. And hot chocolate."

————

Birthday Cake 1946

The night before her seventh birthday she couldn't get to sleep. Her bed was standing in the sitting room now, beside the door to the dining room. Actually she liked sleeping there. The room was much brighter and through the terrace door she could see the lake. In the morning there was thick fog hanging over the water and often the mountains had vanished behind a wall of mist. The dark sleeping room was empty now. Her mother had to get it ready for refugees to move in. Her mother had not been willing to take refugees into the house but a man from the mayor's office had insisted. 'You are leaving anyway,' she heard him say. But he had not been able to tell them when they were to go back to Germany. Later she heard her mother telling Ruth: "I am going to start selling the furniture after New Year."

It was now after New Year. Frau Meyer had been there. Frau Meyer had had no letter from her Waffen SS husband and had cried at first and then sat down at the piano and played some lovely music. She enjoyed listening but her mother obviously did not and after a while said: "Let's talk about the price. I am sure you can confirm it's a good instrument."

Since none of them would be allowed to carry more than one piece of luggage when they left, her little brother and she had got hardly anything for Christmas. There was nothing people could buy anyway. All the factories were bombed and when they did open again they would definitely not start by making toys for small children, her mother had said as she made her a skirt for her doll although she had no interest in dolls. Her little brother got a toy rowing boat that was found in Frau Gruber's attic but was too heavy to be taken to Germany. And the Big Wheel she had got from that German prisoner was too big as well of course. Actually she wasn't so sad about that. It's true, the Big Wheel was nice to look at. It was half as high as she was and had twelve carved gondolas. But nobody could play with it properly. You could make it go round and round and that was it then. "I am going to make some small dolls for it," the prisoner had promised her. It had been a nice afternoon. They were taken to the camp in a lorry and in the tiny room where four prisoners had their beds there was a small table with slices of raisin cake and real coffee for her mother. Her mother talked all the time while Ruth looked at the young prisoner who had been at their house to cut the firewood. They were the only German guests, all the others in the other rooms were Austrians from Pörtschach and her mother did not know them.

"If we are still around," she heard Ruth saying to the young prisoner as they left. That was the first time Ruth actually spoke about leaving. It made her feel afraid as well as sad. Her grandmother had a home in Germany, but her family's house in Berlin was gone. And she had the impression her grandmother would rather not take them to Kiel with her. But where could they stay? She knew a lot of people in Germany were homeless. Would they be homeless as well? Would anybody take them in? Her mother was very peculiar and would not like to live with strangers.

As she lay comfortably in her bed thinking this, she heard her mother cry out in the dining room: "Oh, Bill, how wonderful! She will be so pleased." Then there was nothing to be heard anymore. Now she knew Bill had arrived and had definitely brought a present for her birthday. She tried hard to imagine what it was. But although she tried hard she could not think of anything an English soldier could bring. She knew Bill was not a real English soldier and that her mother had told Frau Gruber Bill was in no way stingy. She remembered very well Frau Gruber had answered: "So, there you are now." But she did not grasp what Frau Gruber actually wanted to say. Frau Mattes once talked in fluent English to Bill and both seemed to be enjoying it till her mother had called Bill and then almost dragged him into the house.

Of course she couldn't get to sleep now. The birthday present kept her awake. She felt sure that her mother would come with Bill into her room, quietly lead him to her bed to let him have a look at the pretty little girl, sleeping through to her birthday with a smile on her face. She smoothed over her hair, bedded her head nicely on the pillow and put her hands together like praying.

The next morning it did not take her long to realise that she had already started to dream with her eyes still open and had then fallen asleep immediately. Now the reality was that Bill had brought a birthday cake with seven candles on it. She had never had a birthday cake. And her mother had been right. It was wonderful.

———

Being Nazi 1946

At school she was happy. She was already older than the others so she got good marks. Her teacher said she could certainly jump a class, later in Germany. She might not be bored then anymore. But she did not feel bored. She liked her mornings walking to school, being there, listening, answering and playing in the school grounds with her classmates. Only now and then it would suddenly occur to her that she did not really belong to her school, to Pörtschach, to Austria. They were to be sent away. Her mother had said: "I'll tell you in time. I don't know yet myself." She felt all right then and sometimes thought about how to say 'Good bye' to all of them at school.

When the winter came again with deep snow around the house and Frau Gruber was sorely troubled where to get firewood, Bill went home to Glasgow, a town far away in the north but not as far from Kiel, her grandmother said, as from where they were now.

Her mother did not speak a lot after that but often cried and one afternoon put a photo of Bill into a silver frame and stood it on the piano. Frau Meyer had bought the piano but would not send for it while they were still in the house.

"I would rather see a photo of my dead son in law in that frame," her grandmother said when they all noticed the photograph on the instrument, "it's funny. It's as though you're a widow all over again. After less than a year."

It frightened her to hear her mother's outburst then: "I love him. We promised each other to keep in touch. We even talked about my living in Scotland in the near future."

"With your children, of course," her grandmother added, raising her eyebrows.

She noticed her mother was embarrassed now and in a voice that was unsteady said: "In his civilian life Bill is only a small bank employee. All of a sudden to have to support a whole family won't be easy."

There was a long silence then. Ruth left the dining room saying she had to do something in the kitchen, her little brother followed her. After a while her grandmother sighed , then said, nodding with each word: "And there will be your past."

"My past?" Her mother's face now took on the rebellious look she knew so well.

"A short while ago you were the proud wife of a Waffen-SS officer."

Her grandmother's words made her decide to join Ruth straightaway in the kitchen. But before she closed the door behind her she could not help hearing her mother's answer which was like a stone being hurled after her: "The Waffen-SS men were good fighting men like the Wehrmacht. Do you hear me, my dear mother? They did not make the war. They had nothing to do with that business with the Jews. And I am not responsible anyway. I am a mother of three, decorated for my services to the Reich with the Mothercross."

She did not close the door now. She was confident that as usual her grandmother would find an answer to her mother's hateful words. But she was aware too that, as so often, she would have to store away those words in her head to try to understand them when she was more grown up.

"I see," her grandmother was already replying, "yes, that

really is something to be proud of. I am sure nobody in the whole world will ever forget the Third Reich."

———

Last Days 1946

The bicycle which had belonged to her sister and which she so loved to ride was given away while she was at school. This sudden incident was a reminder that her time at the Villa Caprice was coming to an end. She couldn't help shedding some tears although she was not sure what the real reason was for her sadness.

"Come on," her mother said, "I sold our dining table and the oak bench this morning. Herr Rausch won't take anything either before we go."

"Will I get a new one in Germany?" she asked.

"Ha, where would I get the money to buy one?" Her mother looked at her and her tears. Only looked. "And there will be no bicycle to buy anyway. As you know our enemies didn't only bomb houses."

In the afternoon, when she had finished her homework, her mother took her to a shop in Pörtschach. Their trunk had to be nailed up. It had been filled with things they could take with them on the journey. The man in the shop was friendly, but her mother left without a word after he told them it would be two weeks before he would have any nails. Ruth was sorting clothes on the kitchen table when they got home and her mother addressed her angrily: "That man who is running the hardware shop now is definitely a Jew. Are they back already?"

She wondered why Ruth blushed and did not look up. She had long known that her mother did not like Jews and had often blamed them for being unfair to Germany.

She left the room to find her brother. He was with her grandmother and was just listening to an explanation of why some children passing the Villa had shouted down the drive 'Intruder'. Her grandmother told them a story about a boy who always said bad things but wasn't really a bad fellow at all. This boy was only repeating what he had heard adults say. And these adults sometimes had reasons for being agitated and then couldn't always find the right words to explain their feelings.

Some tranquil days followed. She enjoyed school. Her teacher gave her a notebook as a gift, made from smooth white paper. She could write on it better than on the rough one her sister had owned.

Frau Gruber said: "Spring is in the air. Hopefully we'll get a good summer." Immediately she thought of swimming. Her big wish was to be able to swim over to the peninsula without the safety belt. But the boat was gone. Ruth would not be able to bring her back.

"Come, have a piece of bread," Frau Gruber said. She felt hungry as always and ate two slices. With butter and Frau Gruber's best jam.

"I'll miss you," Frau Gruber went on after she had got some milk as well, "I can't believe that in two days you will be gone."

The words disturbed her. "What do you mean?" she asked, although she told herself that she knew exactly what Frau Gruber had said. That was why she pulled herself together and asked as calmly as she could: "In two days? How do you know?"

"That's right. Your mother got the news yesterday and showed me the letter this morning as she left for Pörtschach.

Your family will be picked up at the market place the day after tomorrow."

Now she had to think quickly. To get things sorted out. In no way was she going to let Frau Gruber see that her mother did not trust her. But once again her mother had told someone else the bad news before telling the very person who it most concerned. Her sister had known about Heinrich's death before Ruth was told and now Frau Gruber knew already that her time here was up. And it was after five o'clock in the afternoon. There had been loads of time for her mother...

Now, in her mind, she started to confront her mother with a great many questions, sad ones and even aggressive ones. But when she met her later she only stared at her with what she hoped were reproachful eyes. Her mother said quietly: "Come in, supper is ready," and started a conversation with Ruth about a woman in Pörtschach. Nobody mentioned the message that had come the day before. Her grandmother kept her head low over the table. She was not hungry and gave more than half of her portion of potatoes to her little brother. She had eaten bread at Frau Gruber's after all. Then she ate slowly to avoid questions.

It was another two hours before her mother got round to talking to her and her little brother. "I got a letter from the Office for Germans from the Reich," her mother said as she sorted her little brother's clothes beside their beds. "So that's it now. We are leaving. Just two more sleeps. Then we are off. I must say I am happy about it now. People here are treating us too badly."

At first, because she was so well prepared to hear the news, she did not react in any way. Her little brother said: "Are we going by train? And can I bring my toy rowing boat?"

"We can only bring one piece of luggage each. There

won't be any room for it."

"And the train..?" Her little brother started to cry .

"Of course we will go by train," her mother said, "It will be a very long journey to the north of Germany. There are bits of track missing all over the place. The train will only go very slowly."

Not until her mother was going to leave the room did she force herself to respond to what she had just heard with the question: "So I have one day left at school? One day to say good bye?"

Her mother stepped back into the room and shook her head: "There is no need to go to school again. I called in there this morning. I watched you doing PE. Then I collected your papers. That's it. They know perfectly well now that you've finished."

"But I have to go and..." Of course she wouldn't get anywhere with her small, timid voice and...

"No need for that," her mother was already talking again. "These people don't like us. Why do them the courtesy? By the way, you've got good marks. I told them I know I have intelligent children."

———

Departure 1946

Frau Gruber had been right. Spring was in the air. The morning of her departure greeted her with warm sunshine. Birds were singing in the Big Tree. She hadn't slept much because the adults had been up almost all night. There was something like breakfast in the kitchen. But there was no one to sit down with her and her little brother. Her mother and Ruth were hurrying up and down the drive bringing luggage to the roadside. The trunks that weren't yet nailed down properly were very heavy and her mother was angry with all the Austrians for giving them no help at all. From the kitchen window she saw her grandmother talking to Herr and Frau Mattes and then the three of them hugged each other. Frau Gruber approached her mother and Ruth with a small parcel but her mother seemed not to have the time for a talk. Ruth wiped her eyes after a hug from Frau Gruber but quickly returned to pick up the last suitcases at the corner of the house.

She went to the lake to say good bye. To her the water's surface seemed calmer than usual. The sun was throwing little stars on top of the soft waves. In the distance the Karawanken Mountains looked like they were rising directly from the shore of the Woerthersee. There was still snow on the peaks. This year she would not watch it melting bit by bit.

The Gauleiter's summer house was out of sight. A big cloud was covering it. Nor could she hear any voices from the peninsula. That family had gone long before the English arrived. Around that time her mother had come home from the shop in

Pörtschach crying because Hitler was dead. Her grandmother and Ruth had not cried. Nor did Frau Gruber or Herr and Frau Mattes. At the time she had the impression the only person who cared about the Führer being dead was her mother. She herself had never liked the photo of the Führer and his voice on the radio had filled her with anxiety.

"Come here!" Her mother's words had the force of a real command. She did not move. She looked at the lake. Then decided on the instant that she would not leave the Villa Caprice voluntarily. Her mother would have to come and take her away. She was going to show her mother that she had feelings as well.

"Come on. You are the last!" There was this angry shouting again. Her mother did not approach her but instead went up the drive with the sack of potatoes they had got from Farmer Franz for the journey.

She spotted the terrace door open and went into the house. Frau Mattes' voice came to her from the balcony: "Bye bye, my girl." Frau Mattes had already said good bye to her the night before and brought her some biscuits. Although she had never seen such a fine assortment of biscuits, her mother had remarked later: "I could hardly bring myself to say 'Thank you'. That woman is so happy to see us going."

"No wonder," her grandmother answered with a glint in her eyes, "I'd be shouting with joy as well to get my house back."

It was clear to her that her grandmother was not at all sad to be leaving Pörtschach. Her grandmother was going home and had been waiting a long time for this moment.

Her footsteps in the house sounded different. She looked into the kitchen. It looked as it always did. The pots and pans ready to be used on the cooker. She went into the dining room where the furniture also stood as always. But Bill's photo was gone, as were some other small things, including Hitler's book on the shelf over the bench at the table. The Big Wheel was still in its place on the window sill. Behind it the lake glittered in the full sun. She positioned herself in front of the toy with her back to the door. Her idea was to pretend to be terribly sad about having to leave this present behind. To show that she was sad too and wanted it noticed. The truth was it wasn't only her mother who suffered all the time.

She stood looking out at the lake rather than at the Big Wheel and had to wait a while till she heard her mother calling again and again. The voice came nearer and eventually her mother entered the room.

"What are you doing here?"

She was used to this strong, excited voice. These days it was almost her mother's normal voice. She did not answer.

"Come on now!" It was a command again. "The Werners have arrived. We are all waiting for you!"

She did not move. She spotted a small boat on the lake. Two people were rowing and a third was standing up at the back.

Her mother stepped further into the room, approached her quickly, took her hand and tugged at her vehemently. But the voice that spoke to her had changed a bit, contained a bit of the care that she longed for. "I know you want to take this present with you. It's beautiful and I do understand how much you like it. But we can't. I am having to renounce things I love, too. Things that are far more valuable. There, my piano and the marvellous oak bookcase."

Frau Werner, in an old coat and with a scarf over her hair, was sitting on the trailer behind the tractor. Their luggage was already stored away and her grandmother, Ruth and her little brother had found a place to sit on the floor of the old trailer. Her mother helped her up and then climbed up on the tractor, took the seat beside Herr Werner and straightaway began talking to him about something that seemed to be important. The tractor started to move. She was aware that now, at this very moment, she was being driven away.

Suddenly she felt bitterly cold. She shivered. Her grandmother wrapped a woollen blanket around her and said: "Here, hold on to the dolls," and handed her the two baby dolls Ruth had kept in her lap. She did not know that they were bringing them. She did not like them. She never played with them. And now she owned two because her sister was dead.

"At least the girl is happy now," Frau Werner said with a loving look at her. "The dolls are beautiful."

Her grandmother smiled slightly and puzzlingly, she thought. Ruth bent over to Frau Werner and whispered so that she should not hear, but she did: "The dolls are carrying all her mother's jewellery. We sewed it inside them. You see they have soft bodies. Frau Schubert thought it was a good idea. She's only allowed to bring two valuable pieces. But nobody will think of looking for hidden gold and diamonds in a doll's body, will they?"

She let her hand slide around the dolls' bodies. She couldn't feel any rings or necklaces. As the Villa Caprice was lost from view she thought how clever her mother had been. Yes, but her mother had not told her. Her mother didn't trust her to keep a secret. She could foresee that holding the dolls would be her job now, all the way back to Germany.

They passed the hotel, the houses next to it and the lane she used to walk to school. She suddenly wished that they did not have to drive past the school. She could so easily picture herself sitting in her classroom, comfortable among her classmates, being paid attention to by her teacher and putting her hand up when she had something to say. Thinking about how this was all gone now she felt bitterly alone and needed to cry. But as she looked at Ruth and her grandmother and watched her mother gesturing beside Herr Werner she came to the conclusion that these women had lost loved ones and had a reason to cry, like she herself could cry about her father and her sister. But she could hardly burst into tears about her school friends, her teacher and Frau Gruber and Ernsti and Fritzi. People cried for those who were dead not for those still alive. Anyway she had no doubt her mother would be indignant if she saw tears in her daughter's eyes because her mother was carrying a burden, that's what she had learnt these last few weeks, and could not cope with children behaving badly.

She cried inwardly, secretly, till they reached the market place. There was a lorry standing there but she could not see other Germans from the Reich who were due to be brought to the train as well.

The lorry driver very kindly helped them all down from the trailer and held the dolls while she put the blanket away. She noticed her mother looking at her and hurriedly took the dolls back. The driver started to unload the suitcases while her mother stayed on the tractor and went on talking to Herr Werner, looking and sounding quite charming.

Then, all of a sudden, her mother looked down from her height and addressed the lorry driver: "Hey you, Mister, which railway station are you bringing us to?"

The lorry driver seemed puzzled. He put down the old

suitcase belonging to her grandmother and looked up to the tractor cabin. "Madam?" he asked.

"Which station are you bringing us to?"

There was no immediate response. The driver seemed to be thinking about something. Then with a look of astonishment he answered: "We are not going to a railway station, Madam. My instructions are to bring you to the refugee camp 'Treffling' in the Steiermark. What were you expecting?"

———

The 24 Hour Pack 1946

She was surprised and happy that she was able to go to school again. Her mother had not wanted her to go when they first arrived in the camp. Her mother was fixated on leaving the huge settlement of huts as soon as possible. Her grandmother was the one who took her to the school. She was taken in by a friendly teacher and shown to a free table in the long hut. The girl beside her handed her a book with the words: "Take it. I've got two," and she felt almost as happy as she had in the Pörtschach school. It was an arithmetic book. The same as she had left behind in the Villa Caprice.

Passing the sports field one day on her way home, she saw some women coming from the kitchen hut with their daily pot of hot soup. They were also carrying a little square packet under their arms. She knew very well what it was. Her heart jumped. "A 24-hour pack!" she told herself aloud. One of the women looked at her and smiled.

Her family had received a 24-hour pack some time before. There had been chocolate in it along with some other nice things. It was a massive bar of chocolate. "German chocolate," her mother said, " it tastes better than the one we got from the English. And we do need something extra to eat. How can anybody live on a portion of soup and two pieces of bread?"

"There are people who don't deserve even that," her grandmother answered, "I am not going to name them." Her mother had shot a black look at her grandmother as she always did when the SS or the war was mentioned and was cross with them all for the rest of the day.

She spotted the 24-hour pack on the crate which served as a table in their side of the hut. It was caught in some bright light coming from a small window. But as soon as she came nearer, pushing aside the blanket that separated their narrow living space from the aisle down the middle of the hut, she noticed that the packet was already opened. Torn bits of paper lay around it.

"Don't touch anything," her mother said, "we'll look at it after the soup. Sit down."

"But it's open," she answered. "Why..."

"It was damaged," her mother said, bridling. Her grandmother who was sitting on the end of one of their two bunk beds looked at the ground. Ruth said something to her little brother. She was afraid to upset her mother and regretted having started to argue.

She opened the window. Immediately a voice from the far end of the hut shouted: "There is a draft. Shut that bloody window."

"Leave it open. It's warm outside," her mother said.

They ate the soup in silence. She liked their small place. She never felt lonely there. They were all together the whole time. The long hut housed eleven families. One end of it had been home to them for some time now. Her place was beside Ruth and her brother on a bench made out of the wooden trunk and wicker crate, the wall with the window was just behind her, her mother and her grandmother sat opposite on two chairs next to the partition wall made from blankets. Her left elbow almost touched the bunk bed where her brother and she slept on top while her mother was underneath. The second bunk bed was just by Ruth's shoulder. The voices of the people living with them were clearly audible. Even in the night there was never silence. Many refugees had suffered a lot on their way from the east fleeing from the Russians and were not well.

That day they had no bread left to go with the watery soup. Each afternoon her mother would go and fetch fresh warm bread for the five of them. It had to last till next day. Sometimes they ate all the bread immediately. They regretted it the next morning when they realised there was nothing left for breakfast. Her stomach would complain noisily at school.

"Now we'll have chocolate and biscuits, won't we?" her little brother said as Ruth put away their empty bowls. "Because we got a 24-hour pack."

"Only one biscuit," her mother answered. "I'll keep the others for later on."

"And one piece of chocolate," her little brother added, "The rest we'll save."

"There is no chocolate," her mother said.

Ruth and her little brother and she all stared at her mother in disbelief. Her grandmother put the spoons on top of the pile of bowls and placed them on the window-sill.

"There must be chocolate," her little brother said touching the paper from the packet, "there was chocolate last time. And tea and sugar and hard cheese and.." His voice almost collapsed so eager was he to tell them all the rations allocated to keep one soldier alive for 24 hours.

"There is no chocolate," her mother repeated.

"Then it must have been stolen." It startled her that she had uttered this sentence. But she went on bravely: "The packet must have been opened by someone."

"Your mother opened it," her grandmother said.

"It was damaged at one end," her mother said defiantly, "there was no chocolate in it," and after a pause went on: "But, look, we got some beans in a tin. We can have them in our soup tomorrow. And there's some spread for the two packets of dry bread as well. Let's enjoy our biscuit now and then look forward to the fresh bread later."

She ate her biscuit. It tasted old. "You can't expect anything else from soldiers' food that's a year old," her grandmother said.

She kept the vision of a big piece of dark chocolate in her mind till she had to concentrate on her homework. She wrote kneeling at the crate while her little brother played with some pieces of timber and some stones her grandmother had gathered for him. Her mother decided to have a walk with Ruth and both were gone before she and her little brother could voice their wish to be taken along too.

Later her grandmother wanted to take a nap. There was nothing to play with outside so she invited her little brother to go with her to visit the well that was half way up the hill behind the camp. They liked to put their hands into the ice cold water that ran down over the bleached stones. "Don't stay too long unless you meet your mother and Ruth," her grandmother said.

She took her little brother's hand. They passed the toilets which had no doors on the cubicles and walked faster to escape the stench. At the well they sat down. The earth was dry, almost warm in the spring sunshine. All of a sudden she thought how much Witchy would have liked it here. She would never forget that dog. Or Frau Gruber and everyone else.

Her little brother did not want to play with the water. "I

would really have liked a piece of chocolate" he said. "But there was none."

They sat for a while in silence. "Where is mother?" he asked then. "Can we go and find her?"

They walked on, higher up the hill. When her little brother got tired she made him sit down and wait while she went to have a look around from the top. As she reached the end of the path she heard voices. No. She heard one voice. Her mother's. You could always hear that voice everywhere, over everyone else. A loud, firm voice with a note of strong self confidence that often made her feel ashamed of her mother.

Carefully, so as not to make a noise, she bent back a branch of the tree in front of her and let her eyes search. There they were, Ruth and her mother, sitting just a few steps away on the grass, her mother pointing to something in the distance. Ruth nodded as Ruth always did when her mother was speaking to her in this teacherly way.

She let go the branch and started to retreat when she heard a word that electrified her. The word was: Chocolate. At this word, of course, she had to pull back the branch again and look. Her mother was just saying it for a second time: "Chocolate!" Now, looking at Ruth, went on: "Real chocolate, my dear. Look and smell and smile. We are in heaven!"

The branch shot up. She bent it down again and allowed herself a second glance. Yes, there was chocolate in her mother's hand. No paper around it. Clear, dark chocolate. In fact it was exactly the sort of bar she had expected there to be in the 24-hour pack. It was there, in her mother's hand!

Now she noticed that Ruth looked embarrassed, that she shook her head and moved away from her mother. Her mother followed Ruth, held her down as Ruth started to get up, and passed her the chocolate. "You break it," her mother said. It sounded like an order.

Half way down to the well she found her brother coming up the hill. She took his hand and went back with him into the camp. Her grandmother was just getting up, looked at her and said in a caring tone: "We'll have tea now and we'll eat everything we've got in the house. Won't that be fun?"

So they did. It was warm outside but the old man living beside them with his injured daughter and a baby had made a fire in the stove that stood in the middle of the hut. So they were able to heat some water and pour it over the tea-leaves from the 24-hour pack. And, how wonderful, they had a lot of sugar in it as well.

"Feel better now, do you?" her grandmother asked when the biscuits were all gone and all that was left were a few slices of dry bread wrapped in rough paper. And the beans.

Her mother came back with Ruth a short while after they had tidied up. First she noticed that her mother's face was red and then she saw her mother's eyes searching around. It struck her that she was now often able to tell what her mother was thinking. And now it came:

"Let's have a nice cup of tea," her mother said, making an obvious effort to smile, "and let's have some biscuits with it. Ruth may go for the bread afterwards."

"There are no biscuits," her grandmother said in a quiet voice. She held her breath and took her little brother's hand.

"I am talking about the biscuits from the 24-hour pack'" her mother said.

"So am I. There were only a few biscuits in it this time,"

her grandmother answered in the same low voice. "And as you will remember, my dear, we ate them after lunch."

Her mother looked at her grandmother for a while, then at her and her little brother. She noticed the red in her mother's face had disappeared. Her mother looked rather pale now. After what seemed to her a long time her mother sat down on the chair next to the blanket-door and put her hands in her lap. Nobody spoke. Her little brother tried to reach his sticks and stones on the crate. But she kept his hand in hers.

It began to occur to her that she must say something. Someone had to. "The bread," she said, "it will be cold. Ruth are we going?"

Her mother got up, took a deep breath and announced: "I'll go! You're right. It's time for it anyway."

They never got a 24-hour pack again.

———

The Transport List 1946

It was May. She was under the impression that they had lived in the Refugee Camp for ages. But her mother said: "It's two months. Far too long."

She did not feel cold at night anymore. Only her shoes made her worry. The soles were coming off. On rainy days her feet got wet. Ruth said: "Don't tell your mother. She cannot do anything about it. Nobody here has any material to fix shoes.

She was aware of that. There were children in her class who had spent years in the camp. They had come from eastern countries which had belonged to the Deutsche Reich. As the enemy came nearer the people fled. Now they did not know what happened to their houses, their farms and their animals, even to a grandfather who was too old to join the trek. Some of these children wore sandals made from tyres on their bare feet.

Although she often thought of this grandfather who was now alone and would definitely not get help from the Russians she did not feel so bad anymore.

"The sun is making life better," her grandmother said.

"Not mine," her mother protested, "I feel awful in this place."

"Who does not?" her grandmother asked and then went on smiling: "But we don't broadcast it around all day."

"I'll get us out of here soon," her mother said and nodded vigorously.

"How, my dear?" Her grandmother turned and looked at her in a relieved way before addressing her mother again: "As you know there is a waiting list and we are placed at the far end. There are others waiting far longer than the likes of us to be transported back to Germany. Better you pull yourself together."

"Ha!" Her mother exclaimed and stood more upright than before. "Have you ever heard what money can achieve? My piano will make the difference."

She did not understand what her mother was talking about. To her surprise she got an explanation shortly after this. As she was up one night in the bunk bed she shared with her little brother, head to feet, she overheard a second conversation about this issue. Her little brother was asleep already. So she could bring her head nearer to the edge of the bed without being asked by him what was going on and be caught listening.

"I told you I'll manage it," her mother said in a low but powerful voice. "We are on the top of the list now. I am actually more talented than you think, my dear mother."

There was silence for a while. Then Ruth asked softly: "Frau Schubert, how come?"

"My girl, money rules the world." There was this elation in her mother's report that she was always unable to interpret. But this time her mother explained her outburst at once.

"I offered the guy in charge a nice sum. I must say actually a very tempting one. He may buy my piano now." Her mother spoke with a touch of self-confidence as she did quite often as she went on: "And there we are. By no means he first said could he give me more than three places. But, as you will know, I never give up. I answered: 'I definitely have to bring my mother and my servant girl.' Being absolutely determined worked. Now we all will leave soon."

"I could have gone with the little ones," her grandmother

said, "Just to get them out of here."

"You would take my children from me?" Her mother sounded upset now. "They are all I have left."

"So, so," her grandmother said slowly and was still for a moment. Then added with a more normal voice: "And where will they bring us?"

"The transport goes north, almost as far as the Danish border, the guy said. In the villages there are still spaces in farmhouses to accommodate refugees. But we will leave the train near Kiel. We are not refugees at all. And we do have a place to go."

"I have," her grandmother corrected. Ruth was not to be heard.

"O, come. There is nothing left in Berlin for me anymore. I can only keep the wonderful memories."

Her grandmother sighed. "My brother and Dolly are living in my apartment. There is actually no space for you."

"There has to be. Ruth will not stay with us anyway. Right, Ruth?"

She did not hear Ruth say a word.

"You will go to your parents in law. Although Heinrich is dead and you never got to know them. Right, Ruth?"

"I cannot go to my parents," Ruth said with a low voice. "Ilfeld is in the Russian zone. They don't let anyone in. I rather would like to see how my parents are."

Immediately her mother replied: "The Bergers will be happy to receive you. Especially because you can tell them Heinrich died for his fatherland. As it says in the letter from my husband."

She heard her grandmother sigh again. Ruth did not say

more. After a while she gave up hope her grandmother would voice something that could make her feel better. She turned, grasped her little brother's feet and pulled them nearer to her body. His feet were very warm.

————

The Goods Train 1946

A surprise is something pleasant. That was what she thought till there was the surprise with the train to Germany. The train was an awful disappointment. It was not the train her brother had been looking forward to so much and she not at all. It was a goods train. Old, dirty wagons with wide open gliding doors were waiting for them as her family and their travel companions from the camp left the bus that had brought them to the station. It was a warm, sunny day and she had heard cheerful chatter during the journey. Now everybody was speechless. Everybody stared at the train in front of them. The train that was to bring them back to Germany.

Only her mother cried out: "Oh, no! They cannot do that to me!"

"The Nazis made deportations with such trains," a man beside her said to his wife, "now we get a taste of it." He looked at her and went on: "Thank God, my little girl, you are too young to get all this."

She actually did not understand what the friendly old man beside her meant, but she definitely knew that they all were going to travel in these goods wagons. She herself was not too unhappy about it. The journey would soon be over and anyway she had decided already to pass the time on the train thinking of Pörtschach and transporting herself back into her classroom and Frau Gruber's house and to the shore of the lake.

Her mother cried out again. This time it was about how she would complain to the authorities.

The friendly man said: "There are new authorities now." He stressed the word 'new' she noticed. But she did not know why it was so important. "Thank God. Your time is over."

She looked at her grandmother who had stopped talking to her little brother. Her grandmother's face was pale, her lips shivered.

"Are you ok?" Ruth asked and took the arm of her grandmother.

"Thank you, dear. I am." Her grandmother suddenly could smile like always and added: "We all will be ok. That's for sure. We are on our way home. Isn't that something to be happy about?"

Her mother looked at them almost furious. "Nobody is happy here." The protest sounded along the platform. "Look around if you have eyes to see. If Hitler were still alive..."

"Shut up!" The friendly old man shouted with a surprising powerful voice. "This is exactly what we deserve, Frau Whatever. Face it. There is more punishment to come,"

"No, she is right," a man in a dirty overalls said, "we are treated here like animals. The Führer..."

"You too! Mind your tongue!" The friendly man took the arm of his wife and pulled her to his side. As he went on some people came nearer, obviously to listen, she thought. "I lost two sons. I owe it to that devil. But only now I dare to say what I think of him."

She saw her mother making a step forward to confront this man. Her mother had this special expression of anger on her face. But her grandmother was herself again.

"There, our luggage!" Her grandmother pointed to a group of men who pushed trailers with heaps of suitcases and trunks stacked up on it along the platform.

Her mother stopped and immediately changed direction. "Come Ruth," she shouted, "we have to oversee this. No, better, enter wagon Number Five. That's the best one. Reserve us space. A lot. I'll direct the guys."

Now she found herself with her grandmother and her little brother still standing where they had stepped out of the ticket hall while everybody else was rushing up and down the platform.

"I don't want to wait here," her little brother said," and I don't want to travel anymore. Can we go back to the camp? They are having a party tomorrow at the Kindergarten."

"Ruth is going to make a nice place for us over there," her grandmother said, "look, they are loading your suitcase into our wagon. We will feel fine in there. And I imagine this journey will become a very adventurous one. Later we will write to your friends about it."

Her grandmother had not promised too much. The fact was that Ruth and her mother had actually made something like a room for them in the bareness at one end in the wagon. The big pieces of their luggage formed two low walls, the wooden trunk and the huge wicker one made a bed for her grandmother at one side. In the middle of their space she saw her little brother's suitcase with a tablecloth on it. She knew her mother was good at decorating and could not stop herself from saying: "That looks great! It is a home now."

"I know," her mother answered, than pointed at a heap of blankets. "They gave us these. We'll use them as mattresses. So you don't have to sleep on the bare floor. How wise I was to bring our duvets."

"The blankets stink." Her little brother was sitting on her grandmother's lap. He was holding his nose. "I shall not sleep on one. And I cannot look through these gaps anyway if mother covers them."

She looked down. There were wide gaps in the old timber floor. They let her spot the sleepers and the stone filling between the tracks.

Her mother did not listen to her little brother's words but announced: "We will get something to eat later. The first wagon is a catering base. We won't leave before darkness. Oh, if he knew how we are treated."

"Your husband?" her grandmother asked.

"Who else?" her mother answered back with a mocking voice, "oh, such a come down! And we were so successful."

She feared new arguments. But her grandmother kept quiet. In the wagon, she noticed, everyone seemed to be eager to get settled now. But suddenly her little brother pointed to the wide open gliding door and announced with a loud cheery voice: "Look! There is someone who wants to come along!"

A man had jumped into the wagon and stood there as he was not sure what was to do next. Her mother looked up and with a now fresh, enthusiastic voice cried immediately: "Hi!" raising an arm.

It was a good looking man and a friendly looking man, she noticed. He wore old, ill fitting trousers and a far too tight shirt. He squeezed an English army cap with both hands and let his eyes wander slowly from one person to the other so as to get to know all these tired looking people sitting on their luggage and on the floor. Then he smiled. But it seemed to her it was not a happy smile. It was like he was asking for something he was afraid to say. Then, after a while when there was a sudden silence in the wagon he said:

"Please, take me with you out of Austria. I was in the Wehrmacht and want to go home but I don't have papers."

The silence lasted. She thought it a frightening one.

"Please hide me. My family needs me. I am on the run since the end of the war. "

The soldier was kneading his cap now with unusual red looking hands. He was burnt, she told herself. Her father's hands had looked the same.

"Please," he repeated. "I am on the run since the end of the war."

Her little brother then shouted: "He is a soldier! A German soldier! Will he travel with us?"

Just as she noticed she was shivering heavily her mother shot up like she was pushed and burst out with: "Good man, you do not need to fear treason. We are on your side. Come in!"

"Stop that, please." The loud words and a sharp glance at her mother came from the friendly old man who too was in the wagon with his wife because one of the station agents had told him to get in. "It is forbidden to help German soldiers to escape imprisonment. Don't you know that, Madam?" The friendly man raised his voice even more as he went on: "The Occupying Power expects every member of the German army to be handed over to the army of occupation." He paused, then added in a more calm manner: "It would be better to say 'Army of Liberation'. Because that's what they have done. They liberated Germany."

"Oh, come!" Her mother cried. Her grandmother made a sign to her mother to be quiet. Ruth did not look up. Her little brother asked with a strong voice: "Is he travelling with us?"

"I can be helpful," the soldier said. She noticed he tried to interest everyone . His eyes were going round all the time.

"How. Tell us." Her mother spoke like being rushed.

The man in the overalls who had been the first to enter the wagon and occupied the other end shouted: "Let him come with us. Let's outwit the Tommies!"

"No way!" The friendly man shook his head vehemently.

"You have not been out there, have you?" The soldier spoke rather contemptuously.

Now to her surprise the friendly man smiled while saying: "I was wounded in 1918. My injuries torment me still. That saved me from experiencing such a disaster once more. But to answer your question correctly: No, I have not been out there to see with my own eyes your fighting for more space for the so much loved fatherland. I tell you..."

"But I did not make the war!" The soldier seemed to be a bit confused now. "I am a farmer. I have a family. We were happy. They called me up. I never wanted a rifle in my hand. I got an order. You should know what that meant. My wife milks our cows now, makes hay and all that and raises our three children. And two orphans from a refugee trek now also. They do need me."

"You may..."

"How can you be helpful? Tell me." Her mother's strong voice stopped a reply from the man in the overalls.

The soldier ceased to knead his cap, folded it and put it into a pocket of his old rucksack which was slightly torn and dirty. She noticed he was wearing civilian trousers. It reminded her of the night her mother had given away her father's clothing to fleeing soldiers. Who had helped this man she wondered.

"Yes, let's hear," the man in the overalls shouted. "German soldiers are never short of an answer. And I dare say to survive such a long time in freedom speaks of something. Cleverness, I think."

"You will live in this wagon for a while. Day and night."

It struck her then that the soldiers voice sounded much stronger now. She sat up eager to hear his next words.

"You will be directed to a siding several times and will be waiting there. Possibly for days. Germany's transport system is in an chaotic state. Believe me. They may give you food and water every day, but...do you....have a toilet?"

A second time there was silence in the wagon. After looking around for a while the soldier went on: "I shall solve that problem during our journey. Okay?"

There was no answer. Even the man in the overalls kept quiet, she noticed.

The soldier raised the right arm and the forefinger and said like being in command: "Listen. This train will leave in about two hours. I'll be off now. Keep this door open till I am back. As you see there is a lot going on here. I am not remarkable for my clothing. But I don't have papers. They will check yours. I shall join you after that. Even if the train is moving already do not shut this door. Okay?"

"But how will you find a ...solution ...to our problem?" Naturally her mother was the first to speak again.

"Madam, I don't know yet." The soldier raised his shoulders for a while, let them fall back and turned.

"That's a great answer." The old man laughed. But she was sure the soldier had not heard the words anymore. He had jumped out of the wagon and disappeared.

A while later two friendly women from the Red Cross brought tea and sandwiches. She had never eaten such wonderful sandwiches. They were made from the finest white bread and corned beef. Just as they all were sitting on their luggage, eating, and the sunset was reddening the mountains in the distance a large metal can came flying into the wagon and crashed down near the door. It was an angular one, as wide as her satchel was and almost as high as her little brother's chin. Nobody saw who had thrown it but she was sure it was the soldiers answer to her mother's question. The can showed several coloured pictures of happy children eating biscuits. There was no lid on it and she could see it was empty as a woman took it and put it upright in the middle of the room.

Her mother wailed: "Oh, no, I don't deserve this." But the woman smiled, gave all of them a glance and said with a calm voice: "Folks, we are fine now. Let's picture we are on a first class journey."

It actually took time till the men who checked the travel papers reached their wagon and were gone again, but not without a remark about how to close the big gliding door. Her little brother's question 'when do we start?' was answered with a gentle look and the words: "Soon, my boy."

Eventually there was a sound of a whistle. The train started moving slowly, stopped and moved on again. She stared out of the open door. They passed some high shrubs that grew at the other side of the platform. And there he was. The soldier jumped out of one of the shrubs, crossed the platform and the next second was in their wagon. He straightened up, stood there for a moment, motionless, than took a deep breath and said: "Here I am. We are a team now." He turned and slowly closed the door.

After a while in the sudden semi-darkness of their clattering wagon she heard the soldier speaking again. His voice sounded almost rejoicing as he announced: "Next time I have to leave you I shall come back with a lamp. But for now: Is there a sandwich left for me?"

She felt relieved. She sat still and watched the soldier eating. He sat near to her. He seemed very hungry. Her grandmother rested on the makeshift bed. Her little brother lay on his tummy and watched the world underneath passing by. Her mother talked to Ruth. She did not listen.

———

Journey **1946**

The soldier was right, she soon came to see, it was a long journey. An almost unbearable long journey. She sat on her blanket. She felt the rough planks rattling under her bottom. Everyone in the wagon was talking to someone or sleeping or else staring at the gliding door which was slightly open to let some light in. She spotted many different landscapes passing: Wide meadows divided by ditches or rivers, huge and small, forests and villages, so many of them, and towns. She had never known that the world was so big. Often she heard someone exclaim: "Oh, what destruction!" She did not know the meaning of this, but it made her more anxious. She asked herself what was to come after these days in the refugee train. Nothing was settled. Her grandmother had filled the last days in the camp with writing letters to all her relatives and friends in Germany, although a man in her hut had said her grandmother should not be so sure that many of these letters would reach their addressees. Too many people in the German towns were not living in their homes anymore. After all these bombardments they might be alive but difficult to find. But her grandmother needed to contact someone who could get her a certificate that would tell authorities that she had lived in Kiel all her life and therefore now had a right to be there again. She learnt that refugees from the east who fled the Russians were sent to various parts of the country side.

"You have to tell your sister or whoever," her mother had said to her grandmother, "that I am coming with you, ok, sadly now with only two children. Aunt Lilly must make an effort to get me to Kiel too. Although I lived in Berlin it must be understood that a daughter goes home to live with her mother if her own home was bombed."

Her grandmother had not answered back then. Her mother had gone on: "I do know very well that your brother lives in your apartment. And his daughter with her young boyfriend too. How relieved they must have felt to have your key when their villa burned down. But they have to make room for us now. And then, of course, move out soon."

"Where to? You have not got the picture, my dear." Her grandmother, full of consternation shook her head as always. "The inner city of Kiel is flat. Not all bombs reached the shipyards. It will take time to bring my town back to life. I won't live to see that. Your war..."

At this point her mother had left the hut and a very silent evening followed.

Her grandmother did not get an answer from her sister. They had left the camp without approval to enter and live in Kiel. She noticed this gave her mother cause for concern. Often her mother spoke to some women about it in the wagon. There was talk about everything anyway. Time had to be filled, she told herself, while the train trundled on and on, slowly, very slowly, or stood still for hours near a field or a forest. Then all gliding doors would be opened immediately and as soon as there was a whistle, twice short, one very long, all passengers knew there was permission to jump out and walk around 'to stretch the legs,' as it was called. The soldier started to run after he had helped her and her little brother and others to reach the ground. Other men ran too, along a path or whatever suitable surface there was. Some women walked. She knew they needed exercise. Her mother said everyone needed it but that someone had to stay and be there for the weak.

When the soldier was back she presumed he was happy. Just for the moment. He smiled at all of them while he regained his breath. Then, quickly, he jumped back into the train and cleaned and tidied up their wagon.

Often during the nights there was no progress either. It was easier to sleep when the train was not moving. But she realized the journey would last even longer with this comfort.

On the sixth day in the train, after they had stopped at some small station and were able to use the facilities there and get a hot meal, the soldier did not come back. She was sure he had left them. He had helped everyone who needed help in their wagon. He had seldom spoken. But he had looked at her smiling now and then and asked if she was well. She was sure he liked her. This thought made her comfortable for a while. It was clear that no one knew where he came from and where he wanted to go although all passengers had spoken about why and how they ended up in a goods train that was driving northwards through Germany towards Neumünster near Kiel. Her mother talked all the time anyway. The only good that came from that, she thought, was that her little brother was happy to listen. He was too young to entertain himself with thinking or reading school books like herself.

All afternoon on that sixth day she was too tired to read. She sat on her blanket and stared at the place where the soldier had sat, slept and more often than not just stood and looked out. She told herself that only one person had left the wagon. So there should not be a big emptiness. But there was. The soldier was gone and she felt a void. At least around her. The others said: "He could have said Goodbye," and "hopefully nothing happened to him." Her mother stated that it was always clear that he would abandon them as quickly as possible.

She tried to read a paragraph in her book about how birds survive a cold winter. It was a book for the third class from her sister, but she was well able to read it slowly word by word. At least yesterday she had been. Now the letters stood there, clearly drawn, but she could not make out a word of it. Everything in her head stood still. She could not think. Just as the words, spoken beside her and all around her, made no sense. She thought she saw the soldier standing in his place. But, of course, he was not there.

And then he was back. As the sun went deeper and deeper Ruth took the empty dinner bag and prepared herself to jump out of the wagon as soon as the train would come to a halt. Ruth would walk to the catering base in the first wagon to fetch the rations for her family and sign on a piece of paper that said she got what they were entitled to. Yes, it was all as it had been all the other days. And as the train stopped and she made her way over legs and luggage to the gliding door to see how far Ruth had already gone, she spotted the soldier beside Ruth. She was not sure first if it was real or not. But it was. There he was, wearing a different shirt and a new cap, walking unharmed and talking to Ruth. She followed the pair with her eyes until they vanished in the crowd that was heading towards the catering base.

Later that night before the light faded away the soldier came to sit beside her and asked in a jovial way: "Did you miss me?"

She was silent. He had told the passengers that he was

held up while he posted their letters and thank God made it into the last wagon with the help of a strong woman who later gave him a shirt and a cap from her husband who had died just one day into this journey. He said further that the people in the last wagon had it all worked out. They had a system that worked well.

The man in the dirty overalls had shouted: "We did not have to make rules. You are ruling us. And I have to admit you are very good at that. Am I right?" He then looked at the friendly man who never spoke to anyone except his wife. The friendly man nodded. And she was surprised to see he nodded especially at the soldier.

"I tell you what actually happened," the soldier now said, "but it's only between you and me."

Still she could not speak. There was a lump in her throat.

"First I ran to the river. We drove over its bridge, you remember? That bridge which was partially destroyed. The river had looked so inviting. I swam and I feel very clean now."

"I miss swimming," she said and hoped her voice sounded normal.

"You?" The soldier looked deep into her eyes.

"We swam in the Woerthersee."

"Oh, dear. That beautiful lake." He paused for a moment. Then he said: "Anyway. We are all in a hell now. No, that's not for today. I was with an angel today and that angel brought me back to you."

"How?" She threw a short glance at her mother. Her mother was packing the rest of the dinner away and talking to her little brother who was still eating. Her mother seemed not to notice that she was absorbed in a serious conversation.

"As I left the post office I knew I had to hurry back and felt a bit worried. I was afraid I'd miss the train but did not dare to run. In my case running can attract dangerous attention." The soldier's voice let her know that he was still excited. But he went on. "Suddenly I saw an American officer walking towards me. He was just some twenty metres away. He looked at me, only at me, as he came nearer, although I was surrounded by other people. I knew I would be in big trouble the next minute. In my mind I heard him already asking to produce my papers. And my mind told me also that in some further minutes I would be on my way to the next prisoner-of-war camp."

"Because you do not have an identity card," she added.

"Right, my girl. And no dismissal documents from the Wehrmacht either. But then there came this angel."

"Angels don't exist." She was sure about this. Frau Gruber had said it. Frau Gruber believed everything that was written in the bible except that angels exist."

"Ok." The soldier patted her hand. "It was a young woman with a pram who walked beside this officer. I think my facial expression told her that I was afraid. She looked at the officer and then at me again and I am sure she foresaw what was going to happen, that he would arrest me. I have no other explanation for what she then did."

The soldier lowered his head.

"What?" she asked. She had the feeling she was in a real story again. The soldier was right beside her, so it was a good story. Definitely. Her mother was still forcing her little brother to eat and the same time spoke to Ruth with a raised forefinger, but was not watching her and the soldier. "Tell me, please," she begged.

"I shall. I only have to take a deep breath first to be able to rattle off this incredible event."

The soldier took a breath in a theatrical manner, then continued hastily: "The woman made some quick steps forward, pushing the pram in my direction. She reached me seconds earlier than the officer and cried out: 'Oh, there you are, my Darling!'. She took me in her arms and hugged me effusively. The officer passed by without looking at us."

"Oh, that was just in time," she declared, "and what a great idea!" She pictured the soldier, the American officer and the woman with the baby in front of her. And she saw the hugging and it was a source of pride to her that she knew what it all meant.

After a short silence between them the soldier asked: "So, was this woman an angel, my dear?" His face showed her that he was just reliving the threatening moments again.

She nodded. Three times. The soldier took her left hand. And unseen by her mother, he gently pressed it.

———

The next day, to her delight, brought more stories. Although not pleasant ones she had to admit later. First, at breakfast, while her family sat almost in private in their corner of the wagon and the train rolled on and on with steady speed, again her mother and her grandmother quarrelled. This time it was about when they would arrive in Neumünster. Too soon meant her grandmother's sister had less time to get their papers. But a longer time in the train would bring her mother really to the end of her tether. That was what her mother declared as she leant back, holding her half-full mug of English tea.

"I am so sorry that you have to suffer so much," her grandmother said with a tiny grin of pleasure, "especially when all the rest of us here are having the time of our lives."

"Stop that," her mother answered in a morose tone. "You are fine. You will end up in your apartment anyway. But I face a life in a puny village, in the attic of a farmhouse where I am by no means welcome."

"You forgot to mention your children." Her grandmother emphasized the word 'children' and winked at her. "Growing up in a village would be great for them, especially after what happened to our towns. And I am sure they miss the Villa Caprice and garden anyway."

Her mother looked angry now and hissed: "Children don't feel things like we do."

She saw her grandmother was shaken and she took pity on her. Then it brought her some relief that the soldier approached them to collect the breakfast wrapping. As usual she got up and followed him to help to collect the rubbish from their travel companions.

"Will you tell me why you were not put into a prisoner-of-war camp after the war?" she asked the soldier while they crushed some paper box rubbish.

He smiled.

"I won't tell anybody," she promised in a small voice.

He smiled, then nodded while he put the litter into a sack. That was the moment she knew there was a good day to come. She sat down beside the woman called Frau Krukow. Sitting there let her see more of the landscape through the slightly open gliding door. She knew Frau Krukow never spoke.

"You remind me of my eldest daughter." Frau Krukow suddenly said with a quiet and small voice. "She is your age."

"Where is your daughter?" Surprise made her say the words slowly. And , of course, with a quiet voice too.

"I don't know. Nor where my younger one is either."

"How..?" She stopped. She did not know if it was right to address Frau Krukow. Some people had tried to talk to this woman. They got no answer. Even the soldier, she had noticed, received only a sad glance. No one knew anyway if Frau Krukow, who read the same book over and over again, was from their camp at all.

"I had a baby as well, a boy, four month old, when we had to join the trek," Frau Krukow went on. "It was all in a hurry. The mayors in all our towns were not allowed to let us flee in time as the Russians came nearer. Hitler had commanded to hold the front. Finally my neighbour took us onto his horse and wagon and we drove westwards. I thought I was lucky when later some soldiers put the four of us on a train. The train was awfully overcrowded. We had no food and water. At a stop I left the compartment with the baby, but without the girls, to get something for his bottle. Planes came and the train drove off immediately. I missed it."

Although she feared she would hurt Frau Krukow even more she could not stop herself asking: "Where is the baby now?"

"He died." Frau Krukow still spoke without emotion. "Fleeing soldiers took me into their lorry. They had water but it was too late. I held him for a while. Then they took him away. I was in your camp. I noticed you. Yes, you look like my eldest."

They stopped talking. It was loud in the wagon and whispering was difficult to understand. But she did not get up although she saw her mother make a sign to come. Her mother pointed to her little brother who cried. She knew her mother wanted her to entertain him.

Wrapped as she was in her own affairs again it took her by surprise that Frau Krukow went on: "Now I hope that the German Search Service will find the girls. On the radio they read names of lost and found children and all the details they know. I'll give them the name of the station where I was separated from my girls and someone may know what happened to them and write a letter to the radio station."

I have to say something now, she told herself. But she did not know what to say. After a while Frau Krukow put a hand on her shoulder, tried to smile and added: "Yes, you have her eyes. I watch you all day. I can see it is not easy." Frau Krukow looked at her mother now.

She was not sure what this word 'easy' actually told her. But she was sure Frau Krukow was speaking of her mother.

Maybe her mother was not always right. This thought struck her and brought her anxiety back. Because she would have only her mother when Ruth was with her own family again and her grandmother in Kiel and she...

She sighed. Deeply. Inwardly. And agreed: No, it was not easy.

The same day in the afternoon the train came to a halt in a small town and everyone was allowed to get out and go to the spacious station's building. There was a hot meal ready for them and later they were sent, in groups, to get a dose of lice powder into their hair. Her mother first rejected the treatment, but both the man in the white coat and the nurse said that otherwise her mother would not be allowed to ride the train again.

Her mother was very upset and declared so loud that everyone in the Station Hall was able to hear it: "I cannot except that we are treated like this. We don't have self-determination anymore in our country."

Ruth kept quiet, as always, she thought. And while she still tried to get the meaning of her mother's long word her grandmother remarked: "Oh, on the contrary, my dear, we just got our self-determination back. Or let me say: In a while. Listen, what's going on in this country now is to sort out the mess your hero has brought upon us, no, upon the whole world, I should say."

She was happy to be in the train again late afternoon. Someone suggested to leave the door wide open. They drove slowly now like they often did. Warm, fresh air was blown into the wagon and it was nice to see a different landscape. A lake, fields and farmhouses built in a different style than in Austria. But no mountains anymore.

"Keep the door open?" her mother cried. "No way. You forget I have two children here."

She and her little brother were the only children in their wagon.

"The children can sit back," the man in the overalls shouted, "there they are safe. This powder cries for fresh air."

The soldier who stood at the door turned and looked at her mother. "I'll sit with them." He stretched out a hand to her little brother.

Her mother shook her head. "I keep the boy. That's safer. You may look after her. She will be delighted so sit beside you. But don't overdo it. You don't have to talk to her all the time."

Minutes later she was in heaven. They, the soldier and herself, sat side by side on her blanket opposite the gliding door. They sat near to each other. She ascertained no one would get what they were saying if they kept their voices low. But they did not talk. Her mother was watching them. Her little brother lay on her grandmother's bed. After a while he refused to try to get some sleep. He demanded to play cards.

"The cards will be blown away," her mother remarked very audibly and with a grumbling tone in her voice. "And we all will get a cold anyway due to this stupidity. A fully open door! An awful draft! Does anyone here really enjoy this?"

There was no answer. She had the impression all fellow passengers had stopped listening to her mother. Now Ruth took a piece of ribbon out of a pocket of her skirt and started to knit a figure with her fingers. Her little brother was fascinated.

"Ask me now," the soldier said without looking at her.

His words took her by surprise. Then she knew what he meant. He was in the mood to tell her his story. Quickly she repeated her former question: "Why were you not put into a prisoner-of war camp after the war?"

The soldier smiled and glanced at her as he said: "I WAS captured and put into a prisoner-of-war camp. It was a camp almost entirely under a bare sky. That means we had no huts and not enough tents to shelter all of us from the wind and the cold that came down from the mountains in the nights last early summer in Austria. But we all were not in good shape anyway after six years of fighting."

The soldier looked at her but she was silent. The train shook and rattled over worn out sleepers. She did not observe her mother.

"I got pneumonia," the solder went on. "Do you know what that is?"

"Many people in the camp had it. Some died." She thought of the young woman who had lived just beside them in the hut. Only separated through a blanket. That woman did not come back from the camp's hospital. Her baby was taken to the village near by. The woman's old grandfather cried as they took it. But now she was in no mood to speak about this event.

"I thought I was going to die too." The soldier paused for a moment, then went on: "Many of us died in that camp. But then...I have told you I believe angels exist. You don't, I know... but..."

"I do now!" She almost cried and at once took fright. But no one in the wagon noticed. With a lower voice she added: "Since you told me your first story. Sometimes you cannot see the angels, I guess, and sometimes they are there in the form of a person, right? Go on, please."

Suddenly it seemed to occur to the soldier that he had

to protect her from falling out of the train. He took her raised hand in his and went on: "My angel came as an Austrian nurse and told the doctor of the camp she wanted to take me home and look after me till I was better and then bring me back. We prisoners were supposed to help to shovel rubble from Austrian streets and break down ruins so that new houses could be build."

"Our prisoners had to repair tarmac," she said, "but they helped my mother cutting wood instead. And they ate with us."

"You see? That happened to me. The nurse and I became friends. She said she knew under no circumstances would I go back to the camp. So she asked me to leave, without telling her when the time came. Perhaps in the middle of a night, please. When she was asleep. So she would not have to tell a lie to the doctor. 'But please, help my father to plough his fields first,' she added. 'He has no tractor, but a horse. I guess you can plough with a horse,' she then said at the end of her speech."

"Can you?" she asked. She felt catapulted back to Pörtschach. "I love horses. I can ride a horse. Heinrich let me." Immediately she regretted her interruption. Her father's horses would take them away from the soldier's story. "Go on now," she added in hasty manner.

"Yes, I can."

She had the impression the soldier just saw a picture, himself on a field with a horse and a plough.

"We had horses on my father's farm. I only got a tractor when my father retired just before I was called up. I had some time to teach my wife how to drive it, thank God."

"She is working with it now, is she?"

"No idea. I send letters home. But if someone has no address he cannot get letters back."

"Was it a nice horse?"

"Ah... Oh, yes, it was. It had lovely eyes and was determined to work. But it was thin and weak. It had been fed on grass only. As you will know working horses need oats to give them strength. The nurse's father had none. All grain he had produced on his fields was taken to the war. So the horse and I made little progress on the fields."

The soldier stretched his legs. He still held her hand. Her mother was asleep. That meant there was no complaining now. It seemed to her the train lost more and more speed. That brought a certain calmness into the wagon. Only some muttering was floating over the fellow passengers.

"The horse could not work?" she asked.

"It wanted to. Oh, it was really determined. But it was weak, as I said. Like I was. We both were weak and the soil was awfully heavy. The horse pulled and I pushed. It was hard to hold the plough. We made little progress. The farmer ran his legs tired to find food for his wife and myself and for the horse. My nurse brought bread and tins from the English doctor and even greetings from him. We all were afraid the winter would catch us before the work was done. Sometimes the farmer took over my job. But he had a bad back from the first world war and could only work a few hours. Anyway the winter came early in Austria last year, as you will remember, and the frost caught some acres. "

"And then you left the family? Secretly?" She expected a lot of excitement from the story now.

"I was invited to stay. Secretly. The farmer explained that in winter nobody would be able to walk over the Alps to Germany without food and shelter. He would be happy to hide me from the other villagers. And the nurse was ready to tell the English doctor that I had run away. She expected the doctor to shrug and not mind. I think the doctor was also a bit of an angel."

"You stayed?"

"No. I was too restless. I longed to be on my way. I longed to see my family again. The farmer could well imagine my feelings. He gave me a letter for his brother in the north of the country. Nearer to the border of Germany. Don't ask me how I got there. But I did arrive and almost broke down at the doorstep of that farmhouse. My lungs were bad again. They, my lungs, and the family did not let me go on until spring. Neighbours were told I was a friend from German speaking Switzerland. Nobody found out that I was a runaway prisoner-of-war."

"And these people brought you to our train?" She remembered so well the minute the soldier had entered their wagon.

"No, my girl. In April I was walking again. I came through Treffling and learnt that sometimes a train left from your camp to bring refugees back to Germany."

"And now you will say: 'The rest you know'," she said and felt proud about this remark. "But we won't say that again an angel was involved, will we?"

The soldier smiled, looked into her eyes and pressed her hand. She knew he was happy. Like her family was approaching her grandmother's apartment, he too came nearer and nearer to his farm.

"I sent no letter to my wife to let them know that I am on my way. Just in case they are looking for me at home. I left the Wehrmacht before the real end of the war and don't know if that is still seen as a crime. The day I reach my village it will be my last hiding. Then, in the dark, in the middle of the night, I shall knock at my own door. Like a stranger. When they then open the door..."

The soldier's face showed great expectation. It told her the story he would never tell her. The story of a great surprise. She said: "How happy they all will be."

He nodded but said nothing more.

She was sure he now saw himself hugging his wife and children and she should not disturb this image. It came to her mind that her grandmother had definitely the same happy idea. And this it made her happy too. Coming home must be great, she thought.

———

Farewell 1946

That evening, when they all had their supper, great as always, the fresh bread, the corned beef slices and the mild, tasty cheese and the tea with it, and her mother just said: "At least they feed us well, ah?" Ruth got up, looked around the wagon and, to get attention, raised an arm. Immediately there was silence. No rustle with wrapping and clapping of suitcases anymore. All eyes were on Ruth. She knew, if there was some important news Ruth would bring it. Because Ruth was very much liked in the catering wagon. Why would Ruth otherwise bring a bar of chocolate sometimes when the others did not get one? Ruth always shared the chocolate. But in a secret manner so that no one would see it and get sad. The English officer even had asked Ruth if she was married. But this Ruth had told only her. Ruth knew that she was able to keep a secret.

"I was asked to bring you the following information," Ruth said with a raised voice.

"Louder, please!" shouted the friendly man and raised from his makeshift bed. He had been in a bad state the last few days. His heart did not work well because he ran out of pills. "Fräulein Borchert, you are forgetting, we are on a train. This noise makes me crazy."

Ruth went on with a very clear, now easy-to-hear voice. "Our train just got priority and will go at full speed through the night. After a short stop before dawn we will reach Neumünster early in the morning. The English organizer of this journey thanks us. He says we co-operated very well and wishes us a good future in the new Germany."

"Listen to that. Ha!" the man in the overalls shouted. He always carped at things, she knew. She hoped he would explain what he meant. She thought 'a new Germany' sounded interesting. But he sat down again and looked very satisfied.

"In the camp beside the Neumünster Station we will be taken over by German officials," Ruth went on. "They will see to further travelling for all of us, according to our destination papers."

Ruth seemed finished, but remained standing. They all went on looking at her in an expectant manner. Ruth added: "I thanked the officer for looking after us so well. Especially for the marvellous food. I hope it was right to say so in your names."

She saw some heads nodding. She heard some voices confirm Ruth's words with 'well done'. Then the voice of the man in the overalls drowned out every sound. "I think we should especially thank our extraordinary military companion for looking after us," he shouted as loudly as before. "That was what came first in our lost Reich. I mean looking after the most vulnerable. Comrade, you did well. A year and something ago you would have been decorated. Thank you so much."

There was clapping and nodding and everyone looked at the soldier. But she also noticed some morose glances. The soldier remained silent as he often did when there was a debate.

"Oh, I forgot something," Ruth was to be heard again: "We may keep all our blankets. The Nissen Huts in the camp are not well equipped." Now Ruth sat down.

"But we won't take down our bathroom walls, will we?" a funny sounding voice was to be heard.

Laughter followed this additional remark. It actually took

some of the dejection away from her.

To her great surprise her mother had been silent for a while. Now, as they all formed their small private circles again and the train ran on and on with more speed than ever, her mother looked at her grandmother and with a flicker of enthusiasm in the eyes remarked: "Wasn't it great to hear we are approaching Neumünster and so Kiel as well? It sounded like 'home', 'home'."

Her grandmother looked up. "Yes, it said: 'Home', to me" emphasizing the last two words.

"What is that supposed to mean?" Her mother looked startled.

"My dear, I think your home is Berlin. I have never told you how much you hurt your father and myself when you and your lover discovered the Leibstandarte. You left Kiel with a short goodbye and married in Berlin without anyone of your family present." Her grandmother was very moved while saying this, she noticed. "We only got a note telling us you had done so. After three months a second note came and this one was published in the paper too, on purpose and to annoy, we thought, telling us that a baby girl was born. Now you call my apartment 'home'. I don't know what was harder to bear back then, the shame or the insult."

She was relieved that her little brother ended this conversation with a question. Ruth answered and wanted her mother's advice. She sat down on her blanket and took her book. As long as the light allows it I shall read, she decided. The soldier was cleaning his shoes, she saw. He put all his attention to it.

She woke up in the night as a hand touched her shoulder. The train had come to a halt. Usually no one in the wagon took notice when it happened at such a time. They all tried to sleep on. This night she woke up. Someone was beside her in the dark. A voice whispered: "....bye, my girl." And something about an angel. She raised her head. The gliding door opened slightly. She spotted a fiery red sky. Then a person stood in the door and covered the red for a moment. Then the redness was back.

She put her face in her pillow. After a while the train moved on. She felt wind in her hair. Someone passed her. She heard the door being shut. A man's angry voice asked: "Who opened that bloody door?"

She knew the soldier was gone. He was on his way to his family now. She buried her face deeper in the pillow.

———

Democracy 1946–1949

Of course, there was no letter from her grandmother's sister in the office of the Neumünster refugee camp. She knew what it meant: No permission for her mother to move on to Kiel. Her grandmother showed the Kiel address on the passport and went. Ruth found a companion for the way to Heinrich's parents. Sadly Ruth's own parents lived in the now Russian occupied zone of Germany. She learnt that the Russians did not allow anyone into their territory and that many people crossed the border secretly at night. Later her grandmother, although already very old, did that too to see the second daughter and the other grandchildren.

She, her mother and her little brother, after a marvellous early summer in Bredstedt, in the loft of a big farmhouse and a very friendly farmer's family, finally came to live with her grandmother too. She had wished to stay in Bredstedt for ever with all the animals. And to go to the tiny old school where a friendly teacher had already asked her name and invited her to join. But her mother said it was not worth it. They would hopefully leave Bredstedt soon. They did. Six weeks later.

Shortly after their arrival at Kiel's station her mother got a shock and it took some time before it passed. It was not from the half destroyed railway station building or the three of them standing alone on the platform with their luggage. No, strangely, it came a little later when her mother had found a man with a handcart while she and her little brother sat on the trunk and waited. It was then that her mother, just some hundred metres away from the station on the way to her grandmother, discovered a whole square of four-story houses had vanished.

"What's that!" her mother cried as they came around a corner. "It's all gone? That's absolutely horrible to see. It was such a nice town square. I worked here."

Her mother looked at the man who was pulling the hand cart. He stood still and stroked his forehead and sighed.

"There, look, right there, was my company's building. And there...," her mother paused a moment and then pointed into the opposite direction, "no, there lived a friend of mine."

They stood in front of what looked like a big, roughly smoothed-out field. Here and there small, green hills loomed over the wide, light green and brown area. She saw tiny, very erect young birch trees growing side by side. Hundreds of them, she thought. And where the trees had been planted, she spotted red and yellow bricks, broken ones, laying in a tumble around the stems. A clean, unpaved road ran through the site where people walked and a car drove.

The man now watched her mother's face obviously surprised. Then he asked in a composed manner: "Where are you coming from, Madam? This place is a great looking place now. Tidy and in a way, uplifting. You should have been here a year ago and seen the women working to get rid of the rubble. Mountains of rubble. I helped too. With my bare hands. I hoped to find the bodies of my wife and daughter. Our Mayor then suggested to plant the birches. For me, I call this place a cemetery. But let's go to your house now. If we can find it."

She felt heavily relieved when they found her grandmother's street. And the house. Between a burned out and a collapsed one. The man put their luggage at the foot pass. Her mother opened her purse.

"No, thank you," the man said, "I helped you gladly. But if you..., by any chance, coming from Bredstedt..., would you have some bread...or...?"

She held her breath. She was not able to foresee what her mother would answer. There was, for a moment, a trembling silence. But then, thank God, she thought, her little brother, who had been unusually silent all morning straightened up and with an eager voice cried:

"Oh, we do have. The farmers gave us sandwiches. A lot for such a short journey. I ate too much, you know. But they taste..."

He paused. She watched her mother's face. Her mother did not look as enthusiastic as her son. But her little brother already went on giving information. He had swung his right arm into the air and explained:

"Farmers have everything to eat. They have eggs, they have secret ham, yes, I heard the farmer say they secretly slaughtered a pig because they have to give all pigs to the department. And, yes, they have potatoes too."

Now she saw her mother wanted him to stop talking. But her little brother had not yet finished. With a loud voice he went on:

"And they can make lollipops as well. Because they barter. They give some of their vegetables and so they get sugar for their cakes and coffee and so they can make lollipops too. I liked the red ones very much."

"Good boy," the man said. He hesitated for a short moment, than took the handle of the cart.

"Wait!" Her mother opened her big handbag and without a word handed over the rest of their sandwiches .

The man smiled. He said "Thank you, Madam," put the bread into the wide pocket of his coat, a very old one, she judged, and he pushed the cart half a metre. Then he stopped, stared right into her mother's face and said: "Isn't it terrifying to experience what one man and his war can make of human beings?"

The man walked away. Her mother followed him with her eyes and looked like she was considering something. Again they were alone with their luggage. She shivered. Although it was summer it was cold and dark in the street. The high houses opposite blocked the sun. The lake came to her mind. Immediately she forbid herself to think of it now.

Her mother said: "Better the two of you wait here. I'll go upstairs to announce that we have arrived. Can't wait so see if any letters from Bill are there."

Just that moment they heard her grandmother's voice from high above their heads: "Hello! Welcome."

She looked up. She saw a window open and her grandmother waving. Her grandmother looked straight at her, she realised, and added: "Darling, I am coming."

'Again I am beginning a new life.' The line ran through her mind as she slowly counted with the help of her fingers which number she should give to this start. She came to number six and then there was her grandmother already hugging her.

The four of them lived in the bedroom of the apartment then. In the two other rooms were her grandmother's brother, who ran his factory from there, and his daughter Dolly with her boyfriend, a serious casualty of the war. Luckily Aunt Dolly had saved her grand piano after their house was bombed. That beautiful instrument now stood in the sitting room beside the office desk and Aunt Dolly gave piano lessons almost all day. Which was great because she loved piano music very much.

She survived the cold winter in their room with no heating. She enjoyed walking on the frozen harbour of Kiel. Her hunger was quenched by a daily warm meal at school, donated by the occupier's families. Sometimes she even got hot chocolate and a warm sweet roll. She would have liked to be able to say 'thank you' to these people.

Only the further wailing from her mother about loss was what made her restless.

"There are women out there in America and England and in Russia, everywhere, who feel just like you," her grandmother one day shouted, "think of that side of your war. And ask yourself why these women have to suffer."

Her mother then looked at the photo of the Scottish man that hung on the wall. Letters from Bill did not come anymore. Although her mother once a week went to the translation office to get a letter to Bill translated into English and sent it immediately to Scotland where Bill now worked in the bank again. There was no photo of her father in their room. She did not dare to ask to see one.

Other letters arrived. Ruth wrote that she was engaged to Heinrich's brother now and that they were very happy. And Ruth's friend in Austria had married the boyfriend who first had not sent a note after his departure. Frau Gruber was fine and so was Frau Mattes, Ruth had heard in a letter from Frau Gruber's eldest daughter. And the best news was that her teacher back in the school of Pörtschach sent greetings particularly to her. But Ruth's parents had a bad time in their Russian zone and could not be visited.

Family Werner told her mother in a long letter that they all were fine, including the horses Eva and Egon. And as her mother went on reading aloud what the Werners had to tell, suddenly her mother burst out with: "That's vengeance!" and ran out of the kitchen.

"What do you expect?" her grandmother shouted after her.

"Frau Werner says that your sister was taken from the Pörtschach town cemetery to a war cemetery and laid to rest there," her grandmother explained." Her grave is marked with a proper cross now and a metal sheet with her name on it. I think it's a fair procedure. But we do understand your mother's grieving. Don't we?"

Her little brother nodded vehemently and declared: "Yes, it is all too much for her."

Her grandmother smiled. Only a bit, she noticed, and then occupied herself with making 'sweet slices' for the three of them. Which was easy. She had to cut some slices from the bread her mother had got in the morning for four bread stamps. With a teaspoon she then spread drops of cold grain coffee over it, topped it with some brown sugar and the treat was ready. Her grandmother now smiled, actually happy as they ate, and told a story about the dog her great grandmother had once owned. The dog had swum across the harbour of Kiel to meet the family on their outing when he was left at home alone.

"Our dog swam fabulously as well." Her little brother remarked. "And it brought sticks back. Even if I threw them far into the lake."

"I know," her grandmother answered. "But we had no food for it anymore."

A very special treat she and her little brother expected

the night their mother went to the black market too. It was the first time her mother would go. People had told her mother there was everything you wished for if you had something to give away that others wanted. She knew the black market was illegal. The English occupier controlled dark places, parks and end of streets where they thought this bartering was going on. She had listened as a neighbour explained to her grandmother how it worked. "You have to behave very normally," he said with a raised forefinger. "You hide whatever you brought under your coat, like so, and wander about. Someone you can barely see will pass near you and whisper 'baby clothes' or 'woman's shoes' or '1 kilo of ham.' Then he will walk on. If you want baby clothes, or the other things, you try to pick out this person again in the dark crowd, pretending to be there only by accident. This time you whisper for example: 'A man's watch' or '2 kilos of white flour' or 'scented soap' and walk on. If that person wants to make a deal he will meet you again and you secretly exchange things."

"I need shoes and chocolate," her little brother said with a demanding voice when their mother sent him and her to bed earlier than usual because of the black market, "my shoes now have a second hole. A huge one. They look like sieves now, the boy from opposite says. And I wish for a surprise and she also wants one and she needs writing paper that is smooth and does not let the ink run over the whole place."

"Yes," she said, "he is right, that would be great. And white bread would be wonderful too." She hated the bread made from corn. "Or let's have the surprise."

"A surprise is fine with me," her little brother added. "I have forgotten already how chocolate tastes. And you don't know anyway how long my feet are already!"

Her mother smiled. It's anticipation, she reckoned. Her mother looked very friendly that moment.

Then her grandmother appeared in the door frame and said: "And be careful. What you are going to do is prohibited. Remember you have two children."

"I am aware of that all the time," her mother answered. "It's the reason why I risk it." She noticed that her mother's face suddenly was very red. "I repeat I am doing all this mainly for them."

Now her grandmother looked like hiding some secret thoughts but asked without emotion: "May I now eventually know what you are going to give away?"

"The field glasses."

These three words triggered a yell from her little brother. "Not father's glasses. No," he cried. "They are mine. You gave them to me."

"I lent them to you," her mother corrected and added: "Sleep now, the two of you," and left the room so that her grandmother also had to retreat to the kitchen.

She knew why her mother was not interested in this conversation anymore. Her mother wanted to be liked by her children who had not shown due gratitude just minutes before the dangerous task. These thoughts made her unhappy until her own anticipation returned. Tomorrow there would be a treat. A special one, she told herself, for her little brother and for her. The neighbour had said that on the black market one was able to get anything.

The next morning before school her mother refused to talk about the night. At midday her little brother and she learnt that her mother had brought home two pounds of real coffee.

She went to fetch the soup that her family sometimes got from Volker's family who ran a baby food kitchen. Always she was sent with the milk can. But that was not bad because now and then she got a lump of milk powder to eat on her way home from Volker's mother.

This lunchtime her mother talked more then ever and said that the luck to get the coffee was still overwhelming. When later the coffee for her grandmother and her mother was ready she could not bear the 'ooh's and 'aah's' from the pleasure of drinking real coffee. So she went to see Aunt Dolly and Volker.

She always went to Volker, Aunt Dolly's boyfriend, when she longed not to be in a fret anymore. Volker was able to make handstands on his crutches and was very funny. He had painted her and often played songs on the piano for her. But that was only when Aunt Dolly was not there. Aunt Dolly thought Volker was a bad piano player. But he was able to play whatever someone wanted to hear. Sometimes at night he cried, loudly. She then heard doors opening and closing and Aunt Dolly's worried sounding voice.

Today Volker was on his own. He sat in an armchair reading, his crutches leaned against his knee. His artificial leg that he never put on stood behind his bed. It looked strange, the naked leg with the polished black shoe on it.

"Hi, little girl!" Volker said. "Sit down. You are right in time for a chat. I have to know your opinion. I am unable to decide whether I am going back to university to finish my law studies or take an art course that was offered to me by the Muthesius School. Dolly thinks it's all too early anyway. She means I am not yet well enough. But I have to start doing something now."

"You like painting, don't you? So you go and paint," she

said without hesitation. "You once said you did not like the university anyway as you were called up."

"That's it then." Volker stretched his one leg and looked really happy now. She was happy too. He had given her the opportunity to give voice to his problem. Now, to her delight, they had hot chocolate together. His mother had brought it ready made in a thermos that morning. And they went on talking about Volker's further education. She did not tell him the thing with the black market and the coffee. And actually it did not matter that much anymore.

Yes, she was able to put the black market disappointment behind her as her mother, on a school day off, gave her the money for the train journey to Preetz to see her grandmother there. She had gone already once on her own and her mother had said: "Ok, I trust you now," as she came back in time and unhurt. Grandmother Preetz now lived on her own in a small room and, despite having lost both sons in the war, her father and her uncle, was always happy. They had fun together. Her grandmother had told her that her father was buried in Hungary, in the town cemetery of Dozsa. Her mother had never said a word about a grave. She then liked to remind her grandmother of the days she and her sister had stayed in the big house and especially of the one night of bombing when they had watched the light in the sky that had been scattered from the approaching bombers.

"Your sister was a strange girl," her grandmother had said when she visited her the first time on her own. She had agreed. She still sometimes felt her sister's eyes watching her.

Uncle Hans' family lived near Kiel now. They, her aunt and her three cousins, liked to visit Grandmother Preetz too but she herself seldom saw them because her mother said her aunt was a 'strange fish'.

On this visit her grandmother read a story to her. It was a long one. So she then had to hurry to get the daily shopping for her grandmother done. Her grandmother who had been a teacher for blind children had bad knees and was happy to stay at home this time. Before she had to leave to catch the train her grandmother put a cake on the table that had been sent from the owner of a bakery who was able to get white flour. All day she had the impression that her grandmother was very much loved. That made her happy. But at the same time she knew that it would be better not to tell her mother about this. Her mother sometimes reacted very oddly when she told her about something she thought was really great.

She liked school, but unfortunately had little time to be with her friends. She had to bring what her mother sewed to customers and collect the money. She had to queue up for whatever was available in the shops. That, she felt, was very boring. Her mother still had some money from selling their furniture in Pörtschach. So they were fine for now. But her mother waited for the currency reform and hoped for a new pension system.

"Waffen SS widows won't get a pension," her grandmother said, "I learnt that the other day."

"Oh, shut up," her mother answered. "My husband was a fighting soldier like all men in the Wehrmacht. Only the Waffen SS was a task force."

"There you are," her grandmother replied.

Her mother looked like a child who was about to cry. Girls in deep self-pity looked like this, she told herself. There was a girl in her class that was never satisfied.

"Oh, I fell so deep when the war was lost." This was said by her mother in an 'emotional outburst', her grandmother told her later as she asked for an explanation.

Now her grandmother answered: "Dear daughter, you fell deep already, very deep, as you both went to Berlin to support Adolf Hitler. You," and her grandmother emphasized this 'you' with force, "got a good life that way."

Meanwhile she observed, or was told, that German soldiers who had been missing or even thought dead came back from prison camps in Russia. Missing children were found and reunited with their familes. She then thought of Frau Krukow and wished mother and children well. She had met Frau Krukow twice in Bredstedt and they had chatted. And surprisingly some children in school all of a sudden had a father again. Their uncle had turned into their father. Just like that. People whispered it all had to do with Nazis who had been hiding.

She forbid herself to think of her father too often. Her mother was not talking about him anyway. She knew there was no chance that he would come back. But the soldier, she hoped, was with his family again. She secretly envied his children.

"Bring your atlases tomorrow," her teacher said shortly after she had started third class, "we will have a look at our neighbouring countries and learn something about democracy." It began to occur to her that this 'tomorrow' was not going to be her day. There was no atlas with the books the school lent to poor pupils for free.

"Ha!" her mother said, when she got home, "are they bringing re-education into schools now too? It's the occupiers' newest idea. Democracy for Germany! Such a stupidity. We were fine as it was. Why don't they stop interfering?" And then her mother spoke about a Mr. Marshall's plan, but she was not able to understand what her mother disliked this time.

"Democracy is freedom," she declared just to contradict and thought herself very wise. "The other countries all have it, Mr. Schlueter says."

Her mother wiped away her statement, then said: "Anyway, take your father's atlas. It is a good one. He loved to browse and often used to show me how big the 'Grossdeutsche Reich' already was. I am glad I found room for it in the trunk when we were expelled. It was not one of the dangerous ones we got rid of in the lake."

No sooner had her mother said this than she regretted having asked about the atlas at all. Her mother would not stop talking about the past, the lost paradise, all day. But her mother was already taking the atlas from the shelf. It was not as big as the atlases her classmates owned. Her father's one was the size of a novel. But it was thicker, a heavy book with a strong hardcover.

When she began to browse the atlas opened right in the middle. It showed Europe on two pages. The pages made a sound like greaseproof paper as she touched them and were not flat. They were buckled and a bit creased. But the biggest surprise was the colour on these pages. They shone red, almost all over, a vibrant red. Germany at the centre was coloured with what looked like her own red pencil. And this red spread into the countries around Germany.

Surprise made her almost speechless. "Who...did...that?" she asked with a certain emphasis.

"Your father," her mother answered with a smile and a sigh mixed together.

"Why?" She let her finger leave Germany and glide into

red-coloured parts of France, then over the Alps into red Italy and through red-coloured Austria eastwards through Greece and the red Balkans and Poland far into deep red Russia. In the north Denmark and Norway had vanished under the colour of glory too.

"We owned all this already," her mother explained with a second, this time deep sigh. "Your father was so proud."

While she was quietly lost in her father's conduct her mother took the atlas from her, closed it and put it back onto the shelf while saying: "Try to borrow one at school. They would not understand. I keep this to remind me of better times."

Next day at school when the teacher started to talk about nations living together in peace and freedom the girl beside her let her have a look at her atlas. There Germany was a similar size to the countries around it. She thought that looked better.

A while later, when she thought she had actually come to terms with her life as it was, the much expected currency reform was carried out. Now all of a sudden people could buy all sorts of things she had never seen and tasted. "About time too!" her mother stated. "It could not go on like this."

"For some people it should have," her grandmother answered. She did not know what this meant and she had the impression her mother did not either.

She ate her first banana and an orange and her grandmother took her and her little brother to buy ice cream in a crusty, sweet waffle and they took home a real cake. Not the kind that people used to bake from coffee ground, no, a white one with cream and little coloured figures on top of it. If she was free to do what she wanted on afternoons she went to the shopping street and for hours was not able to stop herself from looking into shop windows and admire all sorts of toys and roller skates and bicycles, clothes and the nice books for children. These things came back to her at night in her dreams. But of course her mother was not able to buy any of this. She learnt that her mother got social welfare now. Her mother said that the money would not do and the sewing for strangers had to go on. And then her mother looked at her grandmother and added in a demanding manner: "Thank God, you have a pension."

It seemed useless to her therefore to tell her mother about her great wish for her upcoming tenth birthday. A watch. A wrist watch. Of course her mother would crease her forehead, fall into bad mood and say after a while: 'You know, such demands hurt me. We are poor. And I don't want to rely upon your grandmother.' And her mother really might add: 'I mourn my dear dead daughter still. Day and night. So, please, you and your brother, behave!'

But then, to her greatest surprise and happiness her mother did something unbelievably pleasant. Her mother put a wrist watch on the birthday table. Yes, just beside the red and white birthday candle a golden wristwatch glimmered. It took her days before she was able to control her joy. Her mother had come up with a great idea, she learned. Her grandmother gave the money to carry out the plan. A small pocket watch that had belonged to her grandfather was altered into a wrist watch by putting two hooks on it so that a strap could be fixed. Her happiness was not lessened as she detected that the digits for 12 o'clock were now where the 3 normally was and the 3 sat now where someone thought the 6 should be. And so on. This change had to be made, she instantly knew, because the wind up button and the ring to fasten a chain of a pocket watch were in the way when the watchmaker started his work.

"Am I great?" her mother asked as the watch eventually sat on her wrist.

She was not able to answer this. She nodded several times instead and said: "Thank you very much," sounding well behaved, she hoped, and hurried to see her grandmother.

Some months later, shortly after her grandmother's brother, Aunt Dolly and Volker had moved out and now lived in a new apartment house where she often went to see Volker, Germany got a new government and a new constitution. A good one, she heard Aunt Dolly saying, because the constitution was carefully thought through by the Allies.

Her mother said it was a dictated one, also she did not like the name 'Federal Republic of Germany' and carped: "Let's see, where it takes us."

The words 'Let's see, where it takes us' made her look forward to something uplifting. Something that would bring laughter back into the apartment. Laughter had gone with Volker and Aunt Dolly. But...

Her mother came home from a client one day and sat down immediately on a chair in the kitchen. To her it seemed that her mother had gotten into a state about something.

"Hear this," her mother said to her grandmother. "No, they first have to go out."

"'They', that's us," she said to her little brother.

'They' were pushed into the hallway. But she made sure that the door did not close entirely. The women inside did not notice. She thought she must know what was going on.

"It's an insult. A very impertinent one." That was her mother's voice.

"What?" It was easy to discern that her grandmother stayed calm.

"It is true now. The official announcement came today."

"What?"

Through the now slightly open door she spotted her grandmother leaning against the brass railing of the old cooker in a relaxed manner.

"I shall not get a war widow state pension. You hear that? I am not entitled to it."

There was a pause, then very calmly her grandmother asked: "Why not? Because your husband was a member of the Waffen SS?"

"Ha!" That was what her mother always exclaimed when someone said something that her mother thought stupid. She was keen to hear the next words. She waited. Her little brother whispered:

"What are they talking about?"

"Schscht," she hissed.

No sound came from the kitchen for a while. She put a hand on her little brother's shoulder. They waited. Then, at last, she heard her mother's next words, pronounced slowly, emphasized and clearly audible:

"It is a lot more. My husband is classified as a War Criminal. Listen again: A War Criminal!"

There was no answer from her grandmother for a while. Eventually came a small: "So, so."

After that it took a further while until her grandmother's voice was to be heard again: "That's hard for you, dear. Hard to take now. And the years to come won't be easy."

At once her mother replied, apparently very composed.

She listened holding her breath. Her mother said:

"Oh, I am actually very able to cope with everything, as you well know. I shall manage, of course. I think I have shown that I can be very strong. I have to be now. Again. For my children. They are all I have left."

At this moment her little brother pushed open the door. So she was able to look into the kitchen. She saw her mother staring at the Mothercross. It hung near the window at the wall beside the calendar that showed the month of May 1949.

She knew what a criminal was. But she did not know what a war criminal was. What she definitely knew was that her father had been a good father. Yes, she told herself, a lovable father he had been.

That day, in the evening, she sat on her bed reading. It was an 'Anna' book. The title of this volume was: 'Anna goes to boarding school'. Anna, the daughter of a gamekeeper, had to leave home now and therefore was very sad.

From the sitting room she heard her mother's voice. Her mother spoke, like always when clients came, in an excited manner to a woman who wanted a dress shortened. But she did not let them disturb her. She was with a girl of her age . She felt the sadness of Anna who just had to say goodbye to the little white and black pony. The girl in the book was very brave. Anna did not weep. But she suddenly began to weep. And went on weeping. To her surprise weeping made her relax and brought an unexpected relief. She let her tears flow. And she started up as the door opened and her mother and the woman came in. She knew they needed to look into the long mirror beside the wardrobe. She lowered her head and held the book near to her face to hide the tears.

The woman made a step towards the bed and exclaimed, surprised to see her, she thought,: "Oh, Frau Schubert, your daughter!" Then, after a pause, added in the same manner: "She is crying! See!"

Her mother stood already at the mirror and looked into it with the head bent to the right side. Obviously admiring herself, she noticed, as she risked a glance.

Her mother replied: "Yes," without turning round. And then with a voice full of pride and joy murmured: "Isn't she sweet?"

———

Epilogue

We arrive at Hamburg Airport. I have finished my mother's novel. The stewardess stops beside me. I see the tiredness on her face. But she looks at me as friendly as at the beginning of the flight. I loosen my seatbelt. She points at the book and asks:

"Now you know what the title means?"

I nod. "I do."

"Will she write a second novel in English?"

"I hope so. Perhaps my father's and her story."

The stewardess seems to wonder what kind of story that would be.

I say: "My mother left Germany in her twenties and went to Ireland searching for...let's say, happiness."

"And did she find it?"

"Look at me," I answer, "I am her son."

"Charming," the stewardess says. She smiles a last time at my baby boy who is awake now. He smiles back. Then we leave the plane to catch the flight to Dublin.

Author's Note

For their generous assistance and encouragement many thanks to Clár, Joan and Stephen Eustace, Dr. M. Jan, Geraldine Karlsson, Bengt Krauß, Jimmy Lacey, Anne McLeod, Karen Nolan, Mary Rossiter and Una Whelan.

I would like to extend my heartfelt appreciation to Billy Roche who gave advice and wiped away his student's doubts.

About the Author

Maleen Junge was born in Germany. She worked as an engineering draughtswoman and a journalist. She published women's fiction, a series of pre-teen books as well as non-fiction and has written scripts for animation films. For three years she lived in Central America with her young family to work on a foreign-aid project. She now lives in Ireland with her husband. MOTHERCROSS is her first novel in the English language.